PREY

A Fantasy Reverse Harem Omegaverse

L.V. Lane

To Margot, who rescued Nate's horse when I left it
wandering around in the forest.
To Emma, who rescued Dax's horse when I abandoned
it at Belle's cottage.
Thanks to diligent Beta readers, no horses were lost
during the making of this novel.

CONTENTS

PREY

CHAPTER ONE

Belle

"**D**amn it!"

It has been a testing day.

It has been a testing year, and I'm close to my breaking point.

Gritting my teeth, I double-down my efforts to free the trapped plow.

It's a battle of wills, and I'm confident the plow is winning.

Percy, my stoic workhorse, looks on while I grunt and strain. He's doing his bit, pulling when I ask, but I can see the blade has got wedged under a sizable chunk of rock. A short distance away, Shep, my black mongrel, watches with curiosity.

I push, pull, and get on my knees in the dirt and try to dig around the rock in my path. Shep tries to help—he gets in the way.

This obstacle is more than a mere rock in a field. It represents my life, a thousand big and small happenings that have led to this conjuncture. I convince myself that if I can only move this rock, everything will magically be fine.

I do stupid things like that, try and guess the outcome of mundane activities and allocate mystical properties to getting it wrong or right.

I'm committed now, and the future quality of my life depends on my ability to free the plow.

Time passes. Percy snoozes on his feet, while Shep is lying down with his nose to his paws, seemingly still baffled by his human's antics.

My functional shirt and breeches are the same color as the dirt by the time I'm done. Finally, when I roll the beast of a rock out of the way, Percy lumbers forward with ease.

I burst into tears.

A wet tongue laps at my cheek, and I throw weak arms around Shep's neck. "Good boy," I say as I ruffle the fur on his wriggling body.

I feel like I've conquered the world, but I'm so tired I'm shaking, and I can barely regain my feet. Dusk has fallen over the landscape while I've been struggling with my belligerent rock. My stomach rumbles in protest, reminding me that I've not eaten since this morning.

"Come on, Percy," I pat his hairy neck, and, leaving the plow in the middle of the field, unhook him from the harness. Shep barks his approval.

Guilt swamps me. I shouldn't leave the plow in the middle of the field. My father never left a job half done; he'd have finished this small lot in a few hours. I've no idea how I'm going to plant it, but I'm going through the process in the hopes that it will all miraculously fall into place.

My tears dry against my grubby cheeks as I lead Percy into his stable, his hooves clattering against the cobbles of the yard. Shep lopes circles around us. He's probably hoping for food—he's not alone in this.

The days are getting shorter and the evening wind has bite—my problems are coming to a head.

I take his bridle off and give Percy his feed. He's a gentle old soul, and we've had him since I was a little girl. I can't remember a time before Percy.

He lifts his head while I'm still busy, snorting for attention, and I stop to pat his neck. There's a little white at his brows now. He's getting old.

Beyond the stable door, Shep sits, waiting patiently.

They are all that I have left.

What will I do when Percy goes?

What when they are both gone?

Dashing fresh tears from my cheeks, I kiss Percy's hairy neck. "Chin up, eh, Percy."

Closing the stable door, I head over to the rickety, wooden cottage that I call home. Shep is sitting expectantly at the bottom of the three steps that lead to the door, tail beating at the rough, cobbled ground.

Home.

There was another place I lived once, but this is the only place I can call home. Only, it's not a home any more. It hasn't felt like one since my father died last fall.

Opening the door, I head in. Shep trots in behind. Shadows fill the interior, and I can barely see a thing. The fire has gone out, and it's not much warmer inside than out. It's late—I've been so distracted by that damn rock.

Shep whines and beats his tail against the floor. "Okay boy, you want the bone?"

The remains of a salted leg of lamb sits on the side under a cloth—this is the last of the stored meat. The beating tempo picks up. How can I resist? I hand him the bone, and he's off like a shot.

I curse the little fiend. I'll never get him back inside now he's got his treat. I shouldn't really have him in the house, he's half wolf-hound and meant to guard the site. But ever since my father passed, I've been letting him sleep inside.

Occasionally, I also let him on the bed.

The door slams shut as a gust of wind batters it. I lift the bar into place under automation. It's not like anyone visits anymore. Not since I left that sign. I didn't need my father's warning to implement that plan. I'm a small female, helpless—the kind that is preyed upon—visitors are not welcome here.

In the gloom, I can't see much, only shadows. The table takes up most of the space, the fireplace dominates the rest. To the left of it is an alcove hugging the chimney breast with a heavy drape that can be closed to keep it warm. That's my bed.

Right of the fireplace, another bedding nook has been closed for a year—that one belonged to my father.

I'm hungry and dirty, but mostly tired. I should light the fire and get cleaned up before I get into bed.

I should eat.

I can't remember when I last had a drink.

But I'm so damn tired.

This life isn't for me, not on my own. I'm small, and although I pride myself on my determination, I know I'm wallowing in denial.

I can't survive on my own, and the stores of food are dwindling at an alarming rate. This is fall, there should be grain and fruit aplenty, but it hasn't worked out. The rains came before I could gather the few crops and they spoiled in a matter of days. The small orchard became riddled with fungus before the fruit could ripen.

Then the barn developed a leak and the grain stores were ruined.

I'm running out of options, and yet I don't know what to do for the best. Failing a miracle, which have been in woefully short supply since my father died, I will need to leave soon.

It is a three day trip to the nearest village, the town, another week. I sigh.

I am prey. This isn't self-pity talking. This is an acknowledgment of a fact. I am small and weak; I am an Omega. I am a prize that men war over.

I need to leave soon, or I will die here. But that isn't for today or tonight, but a decision for tomorrow.

"Fire first," I tell myself, reaching for the tinder box. I try to keep the fire stocked since lighting it is a quest. It can take me a good five or ten minutes to encourage it to catch. The light is fading though, and if I don't do it now, I'll have to wait until morning.

I don't have any other lights since oil for the lamp has run out long since, and that despite rationing it. Once dusk falls, the fire is it.

Kneeling before it, I prep the tinder, and go through the motions of striking and hoping. I can't see much of what I'm doing, the odd spark, the occasional brief glow.

My hands are shaking, my arms and back are on fire after wrangling with that rock, but I'm determined. If I can light this fire, everything will work out.

The fire becomes a source of personal conquest.

It represents a hope far greater than warmth and comfort.

It represents my life.

I will light this damn fire. This is a quest I can't afford to fail.

My knees hurt, I swear every muscle in my body is screaming, but I'm not giving up.

But it's really late, and I can't see what I'm doing.

And I don't light the fire.

I try to ignore the bleak cloud my failed quest perpetrates, and the crowding specters judging the sorry state of my life.

Stripping from my filthy clothes, I wash in cold water, and donning my night shift, climb into a cold bed.

CHAPTER TWO

Silas

"This is a fucked-up idea," Nate grouches.

Nate is the youngest of our trio. He's enthusiastic, fearless, and at times a little whiny. If he was in reach of my fist, I'd cuff him up the back of the head.

"Quit whining," Dax growls.

Dax is even less tolerant than me of Nate's grouching—I've had to pull him off a time or two before he does serious damage. Not that you can do serious damage to Nate, since he can take a punch.

"I'm not fucking whining!" Nate is a source of constant rash explosions that have often gotten him a bloody nose.

Our horses plod on regardless of our altercation. The verbal sparring breaks up the monotony and distracts me from the biting wind and threat of rain. The light is fading fast, and if we can't find shelter soon, it's going to be a wet, miserable night.

"Farmhouse should be coming up soon," Dax says. He's built like a bull, and his sturdy roan follows after Nate, who's riding at the front. "Keep alert, Nate."

"I'm always fucking alert! Don't tell me how to do my job."

His attitude is brimming. I'm going to need to do more than box his ears when we find this godforsaken shack our map indicated was this way. We're off the beaten track by a good margin. The forests in this region are dense, and little of the waning light can break through, but we have Nate in the lead, and his shifter blood, even as an Alpha-hybrid cross, gives him capabilities beyond that of Dax and me.

We're brothers, same father, Nate has a different mother. In some ways, he's less than me and Dax. He lacks our bulk and strength—and is far less aggressive, although he mouths-off enough to compensate.

But he has other advantages that, some might argue, raise him above an Alpha.

Some—I'm still going to bloody him good for his whining as soon as we find this missing farmhouse.

"Pox," Nate says, pulling his horse to a stop.

That word would usually instill fear, but he sounds more confused than concerned.

He jumps down with the irritating-as-fuck energy of youth. Not that I'm old, but sometimes his boundless energy is as wearing as his uncensored mouth.

"Pox?" Dax repeats, as a question.

"Yeah," Nate says, all business now. He's stomping up a barely visible track with his horse trailing after him. When I squint, I can see a post with a bit of wood nailed to it.

"Fucking great," Dax mutters. He's not one for whining, so I'm willing to cut him some slack. Night is almost upon us. If we didn't have Nate's heightened vision to guide us, we'd be holed up under a tarp as best we could in the wake of the storm.

We nudge our horses to follow after Nate, the sign coming into view. I can't make out the writing in the dark, but I know that Nate can.

"Sign's old," Nate says, vocalizing what I'm concluding myself with my inferior vision. "Poor bastards will be long dead by now, or they'd have removed it." His fingers skim over the rough wood. "Gotta have been here a year, at least."

I'm not superstitious about the pox, none of us are. It needs a living host, or recently deceased. It can last a few days, maybe a week tops.

Without a word, Nate vaults back into his saddle, and we pick our way along a track that soon opens out. It looks like someone has tried to disguise the entry from view, and as we travel further I can see it's wide enough to comfortably take a small cart.

The chill wind picks up as we follow the track for another mile or so before it opens out onto a cobbled yard. Stables are lined up on the right, a neat little cottage on the left, and barns and storage dead-ahead.

A tall black dog with a wiry build trots up to us The fur is up at the back of his neck as he issues a warning growl.

Nate growls back, and the poor mutt's ears flatten to his head.

I glare at Nate.

"What?" he mutters.

I return my focus to the farm complex. The barn will do us fine—far better than a tarp, but we need to announce our presence. It's against the law to refuse shelter to members of the Imperium Guard, but not being an ass about it usually gets us hot food.

"Dog, not many weeds, neat and tidy," Nate observes, voice low. "This doesn't look abandoned."

No, it doesn't, and yet the farmhouse—not much more than a cottage—is eerily quiet. Not much chance of hot food, but at least we'll have shelter from the storm.

Silently, we dismount before reaching the cobbles. None of us draw our weapons, but I can sense my brothers' alertness to a potential threat. Something about this place is off, but it's not pox, and I can't put my finger on the source.

The house is dark, with no smoke or other indication of life, but my senses are in a riot. Approaching a home at this time of night isn't ideal. The good folks of the residence, assuming there are any, might fear strangers turning up at their door. We're soldiers of the Imperium, and that might add or diminish their fear depending on their past experiences with our kind.

We have a code, and my brothers and I do not prey on farming folk—our mandate is to protect them, but there's plenty who abuse their position and power afforded them as a soldier.

And we would know all about that side since we've been tracking such a party for a month—former comrades who lost sight of our sworn purpose. Conflict has existed between the Imperium and Blighten for many generations. Creeping ever westward, they harry our borders and the shipping routes that connect the north with the south, assimilating lands wherever a weakness is found. And they recruit weak men from our soldiering ranks with promises of coin, which we suspect in this case.

At my nod, Nate heads over to the stable, the black mutt trotting behind his new master. He's silent on his feet. I can be quiet when I need to, but I don't have his level of stealth.

As he peers inside, he gives the signal for caution before returning to our side.

The dog sits beside him, and its tail begins to thump against the ground.

"Big bastard farm horse. And a pen full of massive pigs so someone must be feeding them. I've got a weird scent in my nose. It's making me feel itchy and restless."

As if by cue, a fat droplet of frigid rain hits my forehead—then another.

My eyes cut to the home.

"See to the horses," I say, handing the reins over to Nate and receiving his scowl in return. "Dax, you're with me. Let's see if anyone's home."

CHAPTER THREE

Belle

It's freezing. I'm freezing. I swear this house is more like a tomb in winter. It's not winter yet, and I'm absolutely perishing. I wish Shep was here so I could use him to warm my toes.

I yank the thick pelt I usually reserve for *actual* winter over the top of the already deeply layered blankets, and finally gain a barrier against the chill. I don't carry much in the way of body reserves during regular times, but the last year since my father passed away, I've been strictly rationing myself.

It's not enough, and I know unless I can find a way to make this farm work, I'll be forced to leave.

I sigh and twist over on the bed. I could make it work, I reason, if only I'd grow a backbone and do what needs to be done. I'm the daughter of a rural farmer, I've seen pigs slaughtered.

Why can't I kill a pig?

I tried. You'd think being hungry would sort that little sensitivity out.

"Never name a pig," my father said to me more times than I could count.

I didn't name them, apart from Hetti, the old sow, since I knew she'd be around for a while. And then my father died, and the piglets were born a week later, and somehow they all got names.

The chickens have gone half-wild since I don't have enough feed for them, but at least I get a few eggs. I haven't named the chickens, but I still can't bring myself to kill one.

It's going to rain soon. I can feel the storm brewing, the electricity gathering in the air. This is coming to an impasse.

I snuggle deeper. I'm warming up a little now. When I'm in bed, the real world doesn't exist, and all my troubles fade. I imagine myself living in a fancy home, the kind that comes with a real kitchen where you can bake crusty bread.

We used to have a house like that once when I was little. I can still recall glimpses of it.

Then I revealed and everything changed.

I'm roused from wishful considerations by a thumping on the door.

I freeze; a sweeping current of energy rushes up my spine. My ears strain, but all I can hear is the gentle patter of rain hitting the roof and the gust of wind. I rack my brains for an explanation, something coming loose in the wind perhaps, and yet that sound was distinct . . . *deliberate.*

Shep is outside. Maybe he's trying to get in?

The heavy thud sounds again, and this time I know someone or something far bigger than Shep is at my door.

"Members of the Imperium Guard seeking shelter for the night," a gruff voice calls from beyond the door.

I jump out of bed and stare around the darkened room in mindless terror. I need to run or hide, but I don't do either of those things.

"Please leave! There is no one here!" This is possibly the most ridiculous statement I've ever made in my entire life. In one short speech, I've proclaimed myself as both female and alone. Further, that I'm either stupid or have been made so by my fear! "I have the pox!"

"Bollocks, she has the pox," another voice says, muffled behind the door. This one sounds younger. "I know that scent. There's an Omega in there."

Those words tip ice into my veins and finally rouse my wits. I shove my feet into my boots. A muffled thud and grunt comes from beyond the door—Goddess help me they are fighting now! It pokes my flight mode with a great big stick, and without a backward glance or consideration, I'm prying open the window at the back of the house and making my escape.

Nate

"Ufff!" This inelegant grunt escapes my lips as Silas swats me from the door with a vicious backhand. "What the fuck!"

The mutt growls.

Blood pools in my mouth and I spit out a gob. Wiping my mouth with the back of my hand, I pat the mutt's head to calm him.

Dax is rolling his eyes, and he also looks pissed. But not as pissed as Silas, who's a brooding fucker on a regular day. In the gloomy night, he's a raging bull. Dark eyes blazing fury, and his fist still clenched like he's thinking of thumping me again.

He thumps me a lot, so this is nothing new, but tonight he looks especially savage.

"You can smell her too," I say as realization dawns.

"Of course we can smell her, whelp," Dax says, giving me a cuff. He's not as tall as Silas but has hands the size of shovels, and it nearly puts me on my ass.

The mutt yips this time, the dumb fucker now thinks this is a game!

Despite the blows, my dick is stone-hard in my pants, and I can feel pre-cum leaking from the tip. I'm not a pure-breed Alpha, and that's earned me a lot of abuse over the years. Not from Dax and Silas—they just dish up regular, familial abuse. Despite my lack of breeding, or maybe because of the shifter-mix, I can barely think beyond the need to bust down the door and ravage.

Taking a step back, I swipe a hand down my face. This is not me; I'm not a ravager. It's not bragging on my part to say I appeal to women—most of them are only too eager to offer up their sweet pussies. If they don't, and I'm inclined toward a chase as my wolf is wont to on occasion, I can soon charm my way past any resistance.

I don't beat on doors and force myself on young women in their homes.

Shame brings the hot emotional imperative bearing upon me under control.

"You good now?" Silas asks. His face is as stolid as ever.

I nod. Silas is full Alpha, both of them are—powerful, aggressive, and supremely dominant.

But Omegas are rare, highly prized, and possess pheromones irresistible to an Alpha. I'm impressed with their calm.

"She's alone in there," I say. I'd be able to scent anyone else, but hers is the only presence.

"We figured that part," Dax says.

No one is moving.

The other side of the door offers only silence. Is she listening to us? Has she run and hid? I imagine a sweet little Omega cowering under the table while we debate her fate out here.

"She's frightened," I say, and I feel like the lowest form of scum. But the facts are unavoidable. There is an Omega inside this home, young, *ripe*, and unattended. We are within our rights to claim.

We'd be expected to claim her.

"We're going to claim her, aren't we?" I swallow as Silas nods, and I swear my dick gets harder. I feel a little sick and clammy with how much I need to claim her.

Much as I'm hating how my body and mind are twisting this up, I don't think I will be able to help myself.

It's not unusual for folks to retreat to the back end of the Empire when their children reveal as Omegas. Clearly, she's been alone a while—maybe a year if that sign is any indication.

"She needs protecting. It isn't safe for her to be here alone," I say, and then wince because there is a certain irony in saving someone from everyone but you.

Silas grunts and shakes his head at me before returning his focus to the door.

Taking a step forward, he calls out, "Open the door. We know you don't have the pox, little one. We are no danger to you."

I smirk . . . *define danger?*

"Wait?" I say. I've been too distracted by the scent, and I've not been thinking straight. "It's quiet. Do you think there might be another—"

"Dax," Silas says, signaling for him to loop around the building. All pretenses of civility are off. Silas tries the door, only to find it locked.

The mutt whines beside me. He senses my need to chase—I nearly go, but Silas fists my collar and drags me next to him. "I don't trust you not to rut her," he says, making me seethe with indignation.

He gives me a warning glare before he releases me.

Then he puts his shoulder to the door.

CHAPTER FOUR

Belle

I'm outside and running. I don't know where I'm running to, but I'm moving, and that is as far as my mental capacity will stretch. It's cold, the rain is falling steadily now, and I'm still in my nightshift. My boots are not properly tied, and this is hampering my flight, but I don't dare take the time to stop.

The forest is dark and frightening, but the men outside my home are more so, and my exhausted body runs. It's slippery, and I lose my footing.

The heavy thud of footsteps sends a shot of liquid fear into my veins.

This is all my fault. This is because I didn't light the stupid fire!

The footsteps are gaining. I have nothing left, no reserves to call upon.

A scream tears from my lips as an arm snakes around me. We both tumble to the ground, but he rolls, so I finish on top with his huge body cushioning the fall.

I scream again. The scent, rich and Alpha, envelopes me. My body reacts, heat pooling in my belly. The entire surface of my skin blooms to life. I have not experienced such a scent since my father died. On my father, the pheromones offered comfort and safety, on this giant, they send my libido rocketing.

My captor is monstrously large. His strength, as he tosses me over his shoulder on gaining his feet, is vast. I'm a small, easily subdued prize that he carries without trouble or strain.

I beat at his back, cry, and demand he put me down.

He is as unmoved by my ranting as he is by my weak struggles.

I try not to breathe, to avoid the scent his body is giving off, but I'm panting from my run, and I can't help but draw it in. I feel heavy inside—empty. My shift has tangled up, and the strong hand that pins the back of my legs is against my naked skin. It's warm and roughened, and it's doing riotous things to me.

When I peer around, I find we're closing in upon my home. The door is open and a cheery glow comes from within.

The monster carrying me takes the steps to my door. I see a blur of other men but can catch no more than a glimpse before I'm dropped to the floor before the blazing fire.

Shivering, I push wet hair from my face as one of them slams and bars the door.

Three, there are three huge men in my tiny home—they fill it. I stare at them from my low place before the hearth, irrationally annoyed that they have created such an impressive fire so swiftly when I failed so miserably myself.

They are bearded, rough-looking sorts. As they proclaimed, they wear the brigade of the Imperium Guard. But my father was a member of the guard before I was born, and he warned me that they are not always trustworthy.

All are Alphas, except for the one who remains with his back to the door. I'm not sure what the last man is, but Shep is sitting at his heel like he's found his new best friend—*traitor!*

He may be an Alpha too, but he has the otherworldly beauty that I have come to associate with those of mixed race. He's younger and slightly leaner, whereas the other two carry greater bulk.

The one who captured me is broad-shouldered and sandy-haired. In the flickering firelight he seems immense. He isn't handsome in the classical sense, but his face has a compelling quality, and I become a little squirmy when I think about where he put those big hands while carrying me.

The third man moves to stand beside him. He is taller with a menacing expression. Not quite as broad of shoulder, but nevertheless projecting power, I find my body reacting to his potency. He's the leader; I can sense this. I want to prostrate myself before him and beg for mercy.

He doesn't have any, he is an Alpha, and I'm a lone Omega. I am his prey. My father left our other, more civilized, home once I revealed, seeking to protect me. But he couldn't protect me, and he died trying.

I understand the ways of the world, although I've been closeted for a good portion of my life.

Omegas should be claimed, must be claimed—it is the law. An unmated Omega is a temptation and a nuisance the Imperium could do without. Only with bonding does our scent change so that we don't send every Alpha in the vicinity into a rut.

That they will claim me is a given, it is their duty to do as much.

I'm cold and tired, but my body hums with a sense of fear and anticipation.

Silas

Rain pounds against the little wooden cottage, and wind rattles at any weak fitting.

Even wet, bedraggled, and covered in mud, the Omega is a beautiful little thing.

Stunning.

The Alpha in me would have claimed her whatever her appearance, but she is exceptional by any measure.

She's shivering and afraid. I'm terrifying her; we all are. The urge to comfort her is strong, but I'm trying to give her a moment to assimilate what's happening . . . and for her hormones to kick-in.

Nate remains at the door. He's young and his wolf is riding him hard. He doesn't trust himself not to fall upon her. Not that we would allow it, but it would alarm her if he tried.

Her eyes dart between the three of us before returning to me. They are wary, but I like that she maintains eye contact despite her apparent fear.

The home is basic. "How long have you been alone, little one?" I try to soften my tone, but it still comes out a growl.

Her rich, unmated Omega pheromones are potent, and my body is teetering on the cusp of a rut. It takes every bit of my will to contain it. This moment is a delicate balancing act; we are establishing a connection that will last the remainder of our lives.

"A year," she says. "My father died last year."

Inside, I howl at the thought of her being so long alone. Anything might have happened to her, she is young, and slight of build in the way all Omegas are. A remote smallholding isn't the life for such a fragile dynamic. To think of her struggling for a whole year grieves me. Had we decided to ride out the storm under a tarp, we might not have found her at all.

"I am Silas. And these are my brothers, Dax and Nate." I don't mention that Nate is a half-wolf shifter. The little Omega has experienced enough shocks for one day without throwing that into the mix.

"Belle," she says. Her presence has a softness that my Alpha side responds to.

Her body, though, does not, and my eyes narrow on the sodden nightshift. She isn't merely slight, she's nothing but skin and bones. I want to welt her ass for taking such poor care of herself, as irrational as that is.

We'll feed her and care for her now, as is our duty. In return, she will give us her body, and, gods be willing, children.

That is the way of things between an Alpha and an Omega. But I don't know how Nate will bond with her, since it is different with wolves. I have never heard of them mating outside their own kind. Wolves mate in animal form, and, while he can shift, he could not take her as such. He's half Alpha, though, and the way he's holding himself at a distance tells me the same instincts are acting upon him.

He may not be a pure-breed Alpha, but he *is* an Alpha wolf—he will knot her.

We will all knot her.

The thought of sinking my knot into her lush cunt, of watching my brothers take her after, threatens to break my iron control.

But she is shivering, and to get her out of her wet clothes, I'll need to handle her.

And I'm hoping that handling her will trigger her heat, and once she succumbs, her fears will fade, and she will demand that we rut her.

My movement is slow, but she still starts as I crouch beside her. I gather her up, paying no heed to her weak struggles. Pulling a chair close to the fire, I put her on my lap so that she faces my brothers.

I'm first Alpha and they know better than to interfere in my approach. But they are part of this, and I want them included in every step.

She becomes shy on my lap, her lashes lower, and a pretty flush covers her cheeks. Slipping her boots off, I rub heat into her small feet. Her whine is cute, but she tolerates the handling. I feel calmer now that I have my hands on her, drawing her body closer to mine as I rub life back into each foot.

"What! No!"

Her protest accompanies me divesting her of the sodden nightshift.

"Hush, little one. It's wet, you cannot keep it on. You're shivering," I say. I draw her cheek against my chest while she murmurs protests. An Alpha's scent is potent there, and I see her settling as it begins to work upon her. She is so tiny and precious against me, and the urge to fill her belly with my cum is fierce.

I do my best to temper it—this will go easier on her if she's the one driving it.

Her shivers slow, and I skim my hands over her body, warming it and getting her used to my touch. As her hair begins to dry, I can see it's a fire-tipped shade of auburn.

I nudge my head to Dax, and he heads over to the open bedding alcove where she must have been sleeping when we arrived. He selects a patch-work rabbit pelt that feels soft under my hands as I wrap it around her.

"There, that's better. Are you feeling warmer now?"

She nods against my chest, I can see she's pressing her nose to the open collar of my shirt, subconsciously seeking my scent. I keep my touch light, avoiding her small breasts, although the stiff peaks of her nipples beg for my attention.

I don't resist her ass. It has a little roundness to it, and I find my hand straying to cup and squeeze the side despite my best intentions.

"The lamp is empty," Nate says, drawing my attention from the Omega in my arms.

"I have no oil—or candles," she says. Her cheeks are rosy in the firelight, but she is small and malnourished, and her lack of lighting only emphasizes her wretched existence since her father died.

My jaw tightens. "Have you eaten today?"

She shakes her head without meeting my eyes.

There is no evidence of food. It's fall and there ought to be fruit and berries, flatbreads, curing meat and jars of pickling things.

There is nothing.

Without a word, Nate and Dax leave. A sharp gust of wind blasts through the small cottage as they open and shut the door, and I pull the fur a little tighter around her. This was not how I expected my day to end. The shelter of a dry barn, perhaps a warming stew and a beer to tide us over until tomorrow when we would continue on our way, were the limit of my expectations.

"What will happen now?" she asks quietly.

Only, I think she knows what will happen because there is a tremble in her voice.

"Did your father tell you nothing about Alphas and Omegas?" I ask instead.

Silence stretches between us, broken only by the lash of rain and the howl of the wind.

Before she can answer, the door is flung open. It slams against the wall.

A laden Nate enters, closely followed by Dax.

"Idiot!" Dax grumbles as he cuffs Nate up the side of the head.

"Enough!" I growl. The ever-present mutt is yipping like this is a game.

They cease their glaring match. The last thing I need is for the two of them to fight in this tiny space. Bad enough when we are outside and there is little damage they can do.

The tiny fur-covered bundle in my arms tenses and I purr to calm her again. She softens almost immediately. The other two do a double-take.

An Omega's submission is a heady thing. My cock has been hard since I first caught her scent, but it now leaks in anticipation of the bedding that is to come.

Nate swallows, seeming to come out of a daze, and continues to set down his load. We have limited supplies while traveling, but there is a small oil lamp, and it combats a few of the shadows. Dax has brought the bedrolls in, while Nate has the travel rations.

She watches them warily as they go about the motions of preparing food and placing their bedrolls close to the fire. Dax brings the food over, handing it to me. Her nose twitches, but she pretends she's not interested.

I put the bowl in her hands.

"I'm not hungry," she says, trying to push it back. Doubtless, her hormones are reacting to our pheromones, and she is genuinely not hungry, but she's going to eat anyway.

"Eat the food or you will be getting your first taste of the strap. Nate's mash is grim fare, but you will enjoy it a lot more than discipline."

Nate, who has taken a place at the table, has stilled, a spoonful of mash halfway to his mouth. I can tell he will coddle her something stupid. Dax, despite his gruff outer shell, has no more heart for disciplining this sweet little Omega than I do. Still, we must all toe the line where her safety and welfare is concerned. Dax will do what needs to be done should the situation warrant it, but I sense dissent from Nate.

We are saved from an impasse when she picks up the spoon and takes a small mouthful. She wrinkles her nose in disgust, which puts a smile on my face, but tucks into it without further complaint.

Nate is riveted by the Omega on my lap and still hasn't moved his spoon. Dax makes a point of slamming his bowl down and dragging a chair noisily to take a seat. It snaps Nate from his stupor.

"You don't need to be an ass!" Nate grumbles, but he resumes eating his food.

She's finished. It wasn't a large portion, but every bit of it is gone.

"Oh," she says, sending a furtive glance my way. "Was it meant for you too?"

I shake my head, and taking the bowl from her hands, put it on the floor. "It's time we went to bed."

Belle

I'm confused as to how I ate all the food. I'm confused about a lot of things. There is a strange awareness unfurling in me. They are large, intimidating men, all of them, and I fear what will happen next. Despite not answering his question, I do know of the ways between an Alpha and an Omega.

But I'm not ready to embrace them.

Silas carries me to the bed where I had lay not so very long ago, cold, hungry, and hoping for sleep, and worrying for tomorrow.

I still worry about tomorrow, but I worry more for tonight.

Having put me down, he begins to strip.

My eyes are everywhere but see nothing. My chest begins to heave with the strain of taking in enough air. Is he about to mate me now while the other two finish their mash?

Before my panic can peak, he's climbing into the bedding nook beside me, gathering my small body against his much larger bulk and purring. My fear crumbles under that sound. It takes me back to a simpler time when I was a child, and my father would purr for me if I was hurt or upset.

He's naked, and I want to fear that too, but it doesn't take hold. His flesh is hot where it presses against me; I'm drawn deeper into the nook. The purring increases until that is the only thing I can hear. He moves me to his liking, placing my smaller body under his, lowering his weight onto me . . . half smothering me.

He is so heavy—panic blooms and collapses again. The weight is nice—I feel safe. His nose nuzzles the side of my neck, scenting me as I scented him earlier.

Then he bites over the juncture of my shoulder and throat, and my mind loses its grasp on reality, and I am forced into sleep.

CHAPTER FIVE

Belle

I wake up naked, smothered under a wall of hot flesh. It's morning; at least I think it must be morning, but it is hard to tell since my face is against the bedding.

I have no recollection of turning thus, but there is a beast above me, and I'm surrounded by his scent. I'm not sure if it is a lack of oxygen or his pheromones, but I feel a little dizzy, and between my legs is achy and swollen.

My wriggling sees the beast move, and the mountain crushing me, shifts.

A gasp escapes my lips when his big hand connects with my ass. "Be still," Silas growls.

"I need to go," I say, peering back at him over my shoulder.

He sighs, and his heavy leg untangles from mine.

Cautiously, I turn over, eyeing him the whole time. He is dark of hair and eyes, and hirsute—in all ways, he really is a beast.

Rolling onto his back, he scratches at his beard while eyeballing me back. I have very little to go on as to what makes a man handsome, but I believe that he is handsome. My eyes do not search his for long because he's naked and shows not a bit of shame.

His thick cock juts from a nest of dark curls, a trail of clear stickiness leaks from the tip connecting to the ridges of his abdominals.

My stomach clenches. It's rude to stare, but I cannot seem to make myself stop.

There is a buzzing in my ears, and breathing is harder than when I was buried beneath his hot flesh. And between my legs, dampness is gathering to ease the passage of his—

"Go ahead then," he says.

When I tear my gaze away from that arresting sight, I find him watching me in a way that reminds me that he is the apex predator, and I am the prey.

"Do you need me to accompany you?" he asks, a lazy smirk blooming on his lips.

"No!" Now the predator is playing with his mouse!

I scramble from the bed, my mind scattered as I search the room for clothes. Yesterdays are filthy, and I drag on a clean set of pants and shirt from the storage trunk. My shoes lay on the floor beside the chair, and I shove my feet in, eager to escape the home.

Wait? Where are the other two?

The bedrolls are neatly folded and placed on the table. There are a few saddlebags upon the table beside them, but no sign of the men.

The beast is watching me from the vantage of the bedding nook, his cock jerking with interest.

I'm *hot* and a little achy again.

I flee my home.

It's windy still, and a gust snatches the door from my fingers, slamming it against the wall with a mighty crash. It is still bitingly cold, and the sky is dull and overcast with a promise of more rain.

I rush to the privy to complete my business while trying to bury my worries for what might happen next. When I was very little my father had told me that we would live here forever and that nothing should ever change.

But not long after, I became aware of death and dying, and that was a very difficult time because I realized he too would one day die. Once I got over the shock of mortality, I determined that his death was a long time away . . . but then it wasn't.

Now, he is gone.

I contemplate running again as I stand shuffling from foot to foot at the back of the cottage. I should return, but I'm caught in a moment of great indecision. Time stretches as I stare toward the forest like my answers might be found there. It may be daylight now, but my chances are no better than they were last night.

Resigned, I'm returning to the home when I round the corner and collide with Dax.

I have walked into softer walls. Not that I often walk into walls, but occasionally, when distracted, I've been painfully aroused by the arrival of a wall.

He's scowling down at me. His eyes move from me to the forest and back.

I feel guilty, although I didn't actually try to run. The intent was there, and heat fills my face.

His jaw tightens as he closes the gap, and, taking a firm hold of my arm, hauls me over his shoulder.

I squeal. Shep yips and dances around us—he is a dim-witted dog!

"I'm never feeding you again, you traitorous dog! This savage has captured me!"

That earns me a firm swat on my ass. I squeal louder and wriggle despite the great distance should I fall. He swats me three more times with his monstrous hand and it reawakens the achy heat between my legs.

Like last time, his feet thump against the wooden steps before he drops me on the floor. "She tried to run," he states gruffly.

Pushing hair from my face, I glare up at him, trying to ignore the heat coursing through my body and how his scent has clung to me. "I did not!"

He folds his massive arms over his chest. "Because you heard my approach."

This is a bold lie, and I'm about to set him to rights when Silas interjects with, "Enough!"

His voice is louder than a thunderclap, and my whole body trembles in the wake. He has dressed since I left, but I remember what lay underneath. "I thought about it—briefly," I say, a telling tremble to my lips. "But I already surmised it would be foolish and pointless." I stab a finger at Dax. "And I did *not* hear your approach."

"Enough Belle," Silas says. "Nate, see to her discipline."

Discipline? I don't like the word discipline, it is associated with many and various failings. The most notable of which was when I discovered a stash of moon berries, and my father found me halfway up a tree convinced we were under attack by trolls.

I got the switch, and I didn't sit for a week.

"Huh?" This inelegant grunt comes from Nate, who has also entered the room. He's shirtless, and, Goddess help me, he is beautiful. He's carrying an armful of wood for the fire, and his bunched muscles glisten with a sheen of sweat.

He shakes his head and starts to back out.

I am mollified by this, at least someone is on my side.

Then Silas, the beast, growls, and I know Nate will obey him.

Nate

I am furious, but I also don't have a choice. Silas is first Alpha. I'm half-wolf; I will never be his match.

The little Omega is trembling as she kneels before the fire. I do not want to be the one to discipline her. I suspect Silas knows as much, and that is why he's forcing this. She's petite, helpless, and her safety depends upon her obedience. Further, it will aid bonding her to us.

But I still don't want to be the one who does it.

The mutt sits beside me, tail thumping the floor in anticipation of fun. "Out," I say. He whines and trots out with his tail between his legs. This will be nothing like a couple of swats Dax landed on her ass, and the mutt won't sit it out.

I dump the logs by the fire, hedging for time to compose myself as Dax crosses to close the door.

Outside, I'm calm, but inside, my wolf is going nuts. We haven't touched her yet. All I can think about is holding her down and rutting her.

Silas got to hold and comfort her all night, and I'm bitter that I must mete out pain. Dax has put his hands on her to bring her back twice.

Her first encounter with me will be associated with pain.

My wolf is up for touching her any way we can. He wants to soothe her when the discipline is done—and bite her and rut her into next week.

I don't trust myself or my wolf, but I must overcome my fear for the little Omega's sake.

I go and stand before her—this is the closest we have been. I can see the flecks of gold in her pretty blue eyes . . . and the way her clothes hang from her slight frame. This morning when Dax and I roused, we made a thorough search of the farm. The grain store was nearly empty, and what there is looks ready to turn—a couple of barrels of apples, and little else beside the pigs and a few chickens.

She needs to understand that she is ours now, and the discipline is part of that.

"Ten with your belt," Silas states in an even tone. His locked jaw suggests fucking with his instruction would be a very bad idea.

"No, please!" Her eyes shift between the three of us before settling on me. They are wild and full of worry so I won't draw this out.

Releasing my buckle, I draw out my belt.

She tracks the movement, mouth parted on a gasp, pretty face flushed. My cock is hard and pulsing inside my leather pants where it's trapped against my thigh.

"You can't! I didn't do anything!" Tears are pooling in her eyes.

"You thought about it," I say coldly. I can be as serious as both my dickhead brothers if I need to be. Clamping a fist around her arm, I haul her to her feet. I've welted a girl's ass enough times in my short life to know how it's done. Sometimes it's light and playful and intended to stoke their arousal.

Sometimes it is sharp and intended to get an important point across.

I'm deluding myself—it is always sexual. There's no way to have a woman twitching under the sting of your hand or belt and not be aroused. Watching their pretty ass turn red is a deeply captivating sight.

Her skin is soft under my calloused fingers, and there isn't enough flesh covering the bone.

"This is for your own good," I say as I bend her over the wide oaken table that dominates the room. "You aren't ignorant of what is happening here. We are Alphas, and you are an Omega. You must be reminded of your place." She struggles, but I'm stronger and it does her no good. "An Omega obeys her Alphas. Your father is gone, and we are your Alphas now."

Her ass wriggles enticingly as I plant a hand in the center of her back, and her glorious auburn hair tumbles over her shoulders and face in messy waves. My pants are slipping without my belt, and I swear my iron-hard dick is the only thing keeping them up. Placing the belt on the table where she can see it, I deliver a few spanks with the palm of my hand to warm her up.

"Get off me!"

"Take your punishment like a good girl, and I'll make you feel good once it's done."

Silas growls, but I don't pay him any heed. It will teach the fucker to make me discipline her when we all know Dax in all his stolid glory is the best man for such a job.

Her continuing struggles bring a smirk to my lips—I elect to reward her at the end anyway. Now that I've had her little body squirming under me, my fears in being the one to discipline her fade away.

It feels right—she is ours now, and I think this won't be the last time she needs to be corrected.

Yeah, send me straight to hell, I'll be praying to the Goddess that she needs this every day.

Reaching around, I find the tie for her pants. Her squeal of outrage accompanies them coming loose, and I yank them down with a feral grin.

I suck a sharp breath as her wriggling ass is exposed. Fuck, this is going to kill me. I already want to pile-drive her from behind and I've barely started.

She is kicking and straining under my hand like a feral kitten. "Put your legs down, Belle," I say, backing up this command with a series of sharp swats to the tender sit-spot. It makes her ass cheeks dance when she strains to escape the blow, but she stops kicking immediately.

I land a few more for no reason other than the pleasure of this heady sight.

"Are you going to take your punishment like a good girl, or do I need to warm this pretty ass up more first?"

Her confirmation might be garbled, but the tone is sharp and imperious.

My hand connects with a clap against her sit-spot. "That sounded like attitude?"

Her body trembles with suppressed rage, and the unmistakable scent of gathering slick permeates the air.

She needs fucking and claiming, but I understand my first Alpha's intentions. This handling will stimulate her hormones. It is only a matter of time before she goes into heat.

Still, now, she lays quietly against the table. I take up the belt, looping it over within my fist. Her ass is flushed from the administrations of my hand, but the belt will leave nice welts. My brothers are watching me. They are aroused, as I am.

We all anticipate her coming into heat.

Maybe the belt will be enough to tip her over. Perhaps it will be when I pet her hot, little pussy and bring her to her first climax at the hands of a man.

Or perhaps we will need to handle and touch her for many days before she falls.

It doesn't matter. I was impatient before I touched her, but now I'm calm.

Determined, I draw my hand back.

The first lick of the belt brings a squeal to her lips. A red stripe blooms across blushing cheeks.

"Hands down!" She has reached to try and cover her vulnerable ass. "Or I will start the count again."

With a sob of defeat, she removes her hands, fisting them beside her face. She has no choice but to accept this, and the quicker she does, the better all round.

The next two blows come in quick succession. The stripes are a livid pink, and I pause to pinch and pet the inflamed flesh. "You belong to us now, little Omega." I slide a finger along her slit, finding it saturated with slick. "We will care for you and keep you safe." The next blows are a little firmer, and the welts make a pretty pattern.

I spread my palm over the heated flesh before testing her response. A little needy whimper accompanies my fingers sliding over her swollen clit.

I finish her punishment swiftly—I'm sure we're both close to our limit, and I can hear the ragged breathing of Dax and Silas, so I think they are both similarly affected.

She sobs through the last few licks of the belt, and I hold her to the table with a hand to the center of the back when she looks like she might try and bolt now it's over.

"Good girl," I say softly, torturing myself as I get my hand on the flaming cheeks of her ass. "It's all over now. You took your punishment perfectly, and I'm going to reward you."

Silas growls softly, but he doesn't tell me to stop. I doubt he'll let me discipline her again, and I'm going all out.

"Open your legs for me. Good girl, now push your bottom up."

Silas mutters under his breath—I'm sure he just threatened to castrate me. But I'm committed to the journey, and the only thing at the end is Belle coming by my hand.

I play in the slick-coated tops of her thighs before returning my attention to the welts. Shocked little gasps accompany me pinching them. "I've welted your ass nicely. Would you like me to make you feel good now?"

"May the Goddess pox your cock!"

I grunt, Dax chuckles—the fucker!

Not to be thwarted, I find her clit slippery and swollen under my fingertips. I pinch and pet the needy little nub while telling her that I do not appreciate her cursing, but since she did take her punishment like a good girl, I'll make her feel good.

She comes with a scream, her whole body trembling and dancing, and I pin her thoroughly so that I can wring the last throes of pleasure until she is too sensitive to bear any more.

After, I gather her up into my arms and take her to the bedding nook. I hold her close and purr for her.

I want to fuck her so badly, but Silas won't allow it. So I comfort her and enjoy the heat of her flushed, well-disciplined ass under my hand until she drifts off to sleep.

CHAPTER SIX

Dax

I storm out of the farmstead in a foul mood.

What the fuck is wrong with Silas, giving her over to Nate for discipline? The whelp is a natural showman, and I damn near embarrassed myself like a green lad watching him handle her.

It should have taken a few minutes, but I swear it went on for a lifetime.

And then he made her come, and I nearly blacked out there was so much blood thudding through my dick.

Silas remains in the house, but I don't linger and head off to chop wood.

Other than the small amount Nate has already prepared, there is no fucking wood cut—at all. The chips and chucks I can see scattered about near the store tell me that the little Omega can't wield an ax.

And that puts me in a temper.

I take it out on the wood. Soon there is a pile of wood to keep

36

the cottage fire blazing for a week, and I pause to strip my thick woolen shirt, having worked up a sweat.

I know what the other two think of me. Nate wears his feelings like a banner. Silas is more middle of the road. Me? I'm the one who's not supposed to feel things—the one who's calm even in the midst of a storm.

The wood splits under the ax—I imagine Nate's pretty face smashing under my fist.

It isn't a charitable thought to have toward my sibling, who was only doing what our first Alpha told him to do.

My Alpha dynamic revealed at ten. My body grew too fast, and I was ridiculed for being slow-witted and clumsy. Silas was already established as first Alpha, while Nate bore a shifter's natural grace and beauty. Showing your feelings was a sign of weakness, so I learned to bury them.

I feel things. At times, I feel too much. But it's all locked inside of me, and I never let that shit out. A hot pool of hate, fear, love . . . and lust that is too big for the world to endure.

The next block splits with a satisfying crack.

Except with her, Belle, our little Omega prey. The woman we will soon rut and breed. With her, it's all clamoring close to the surface.

I don't fucking like it.

The next block shatters under the force of my blow, and pieces explode, stinging my exposed chest.

I thought Nate was going to be the one to crack after his reaction to getting a whiff of her ripe scent. Now, I think I'm going to lose it before I get inside her.

I can't afford to lose control. Of the three of us, I most need to contain my Alpha beast and to be gentle with her so that I don't break her.

It would be so fucking easy to break her—and that would destroy me.

The only sliver of good I can find in the whole, labored experience is that he welted her pretty ass well and I don't think she'll consider running any time soon. But she's got a fiery attitude lurking under her shy surface, and future corrections are a given.

My cock has barely begun to ease its throbbing when thoughts of her welted ass bring the beast raging to the surface again.

Dropping the ax to the ground, I stack up what I've chopped, then haul the next block into place.

"You good?"

Snatching up my ax, I give Silas the *look*.

He grins. He's first Alpha, he can fucking grin because he's the one making the decisions and the one who's going to fuck her first.

"Tell me you've not left him alone in there with her?" I say. "He'll be balls deep and damned with the consequence."

Silas thumbs over his shoulder. "He's scouting the area. His wolf was getting itchy. Better he runs it off, and he may as well make himself useful at the same time. Told him to take the horse a little distance away before shifting, to be safe."

I grunt and go back to splitting wood.

"We need her in heat," he says like I don't already fucking know that.

It will be better if she drives the bonding process. Yet there are other matters to contend with. "We can't stay here for long," I say. "We've tracked them this far."

"Are you suggesting that we leave her?" he demands, and although I don't check, I can feel his scowl. She is tiny and helpless. There is barely enough food, and none of the variety required to keep a person healthy.

"The damn mutt is next to useless," is all I finally say.

He sighs loudly. "Maybe we could leave Nate here?"

This is not a question I deem worthy of an answer, so I don't. The next block of wood has a knot and the ax becomes lodged, putting me in an even bleaker mood. I pin the block under my boot and work the blade to get it loose. It's wedged like a bastard, and I finally lift both block and ax and smash the collective mass against the cutting stump.

It splinters and the blade is free.

"That's one way of getting it done," Silas says.

I swing my head his way. "Nate? I didn't take that for a serious option."

"No, the wood." He points at the decimation. "And no, I don't intend to leave her with Nate. He'll be too busy rutting her into a stupor to see to her protection . . . I could leave you, though."

"No!" The words come out with more bite than I intend. Silas only smiles. We are only two years apart and he knows me as well as any man can.

Nate is six years younger than me and half-wolf. "Do you think he'll bond with her like us?"

Silas shrugs. "Maybe. I always presumed he would mate with one of his own kind. He can shift—that is unusual for a half-breed. It's his dominant side, or so I presumed. Maybe he will mate Belle, or maybe one day, when the time is right, he'll go his own way."

I chop the next log cleanly. "And what about Belle? She looked at him in the way of a woman in love before he disciplined her." I don't mention her shattering climax while he fingered her wet pussy or the way she clung to him on the bedding nook as he comforted her, but it's what I'm thinking about.

"None of us expected this," Silas says reasonably.

I understand this, but I don't feel reasonable about any of it. What I want is to take her and mount her like a beast. "I'm half-way into my rut," I admit. "If I'd spent another minute in that room listening to her screams of pleasure—"

He puts a hand on my shoulder. I'm gripping the ax like I'm about to commit murder. "You will not lose yourself, Dax. I won't let you." His attention shifts to something over my shoulder. "He's back early."

I swing around to see Nate ride back into the clearing, the ever-present mutt comes trotting over to greet him. Nate jumps down from the saddle and jogs over to us. "I picked up their trail about ten miles east, heading north-east."

"That is close," Silas says. "How old is the trail?"

Nate looks skyward, where more heavy clouds loom. "Hard to tell given the storm. It'll rain again tonight. Won't be much left after that. Want me to take a deeper scout?"

A deeper scout means he might be gone the rest of the day . . . maybe into the night.

And during that time, Belle might succumb to her heat.

I watch Silas weigh up the options. We need to know where they are headed, and losing their trail is a risk. But we have an Omega to consider now.

I think her heat might start sooner rather than later.

Nate, for once, waits the decision out. It might be too early to draw conclusions, but I have a suspicion that our little, flame-haired Omega will have a positive influence on him.

Finally, Silas shakes his head. "We need food, wood, and water stocked inside." Instructions issued, he stalks toward the cottage— we are dismissed.

When I turn back, Nate is grinning. "Looks like my discipline was on point," he says, stretching out a phantom crick in his neck.

I clip the cocky bastard up the back of the head and go back to chopping wood.

CHAPTER SEVEN

Silas

I'm troubled by news that our quarry is near. We've been tracking them for a month, following a trail of destruction they've left in their wake. Villages and towns raided. Death, violence, and mayhem.

They are the lowest form of scum, and it would give me great pleasure to end them all.

But I have another responsibility now: to the Omega that we've found. Such a rare prize cannot be left unattended. We must claim her, it is our duty and the law.

I open the door quietly . . . unlike Nate, who throws it open with enough gusto that I'm surprised it's still attached to the hinges. He's used to our other homes, which are sturdier than this small cottage.

The Imperium Guard's barracks are designed for durability, while our family home is built on a different scale and has survived generations of Alphas.

The distant corners of the Empire are the domain of the loner

Betas, and the lesser shifter packs.

It is not a place for Alphas unless they are seeking to protect an Omega. Her father would not be the first man to hide his daughter so that she might have a chance to mature before the fighting over her began.

There are very few communities in this remote region, mostly it is small, independent farmers and trappers who venture into civilization only as often as they must. Oswold has brought his gang here for a reason—to lose themselves and escape the Imperium's wrath.

Yesterday, when we were still following their trail, Oswold's death was the only thing on my mind.

Then we arrived at this small cottage, and everything changed.

Sprawled out on her belly, with her flame-tipped hair spilling in waves over her face, our Omega is a vision of the Goddess herself.

Fate is a vague, fantastical concept, and one I would not ordinarily yield to. Yet, I find our arrival at this point in time to be fateful, nonetheless.

I haven't thought beyond my service to the Imperium. My life will change now, and once we claim her, our time in service will be up.

The room tilts around me; I'm disquieted by the changes coming to my life.

I will be expected to return to my home, where she can be protected.

This resting image of the Goddess knows nothing of the upheaval she brings to our lives. We aren't the only ones affected, for although I am first Alpha, I'm the second-born son, and the first son will not be expecting us to turn up at his door with a claimed Omega.

Omegas are rare and never claimed by a single mate. Even after bonding, some might try to steal them away. Usually, it's brothers or close Alphas who form a family bond.

I am first Alpha, the dominant male among my brothers. I will be the one who holds autonomy over her care, discipline, and fucking rights.

A grin splits my face—Bram will not be pleased. He'll need to yield to me if he wants access to Belle.

Belle

I have been left alone for mere moments when the beast returns to the cottage. He is trying to be quiet, but I know that he's there. I'm awakened to his scent—to all their smells. He might as well have slammed the door against the wall like Nate does every time he comes in or out.

I can sense him watching me, but I'm facing away and pretend to be asleep.

Maybe he will go away.

They have stoked the fire so that it is toasty warm despite the bitter chill of the autumn wind. But the door opening has brought a blast of frigid air, and goosebumps erupt all over my skin.

Silas comes straight over to the bedding nook, kicks off his boots, and climbs in fully dressed.

I squeal when his big hand closes over my calf, stilling my flight.

Why hadn't I gotten up?

"Let me see," he says gruffly. I'm given no opportunity to work out what this request pertains to before I'm flipped onto my stomach.

His big hand is on my bottom, which is hot and sore, and I complain bitterly until he spanks it hard enough to send every tender nerve screaming to life.

"Be still," Silas commands. "I want to inspect your well-disciplined ass."

His inspection involves much squeezing of the tender flesh.

Every pinch reawakens more of the pain, and for reasons that I can't explain, it drives more dampness between my legs.

I try to keep my legs together—he insists I open them.

I don't want another spanking so I do as I'm told.

His scent envelops me the longer he remains beside me. It merges to that of Nate, and even a little lingering hint of Dax. As the minutes pass, his touch gentles, and my awareness shifts from discomfort to need.

This is a foreign feeling for me—it is like their presence has awoken me.

His fingers are a vortex that sucks in all my thoughts. Hands skim lightly over sensitive skin, dipping between my thighs to find the stickiness pooling there. I should be ashamed, but I'm feeling languid and a little dizzy.

"Do you want me to make you feel good like Nate did?" he asks.

"Yes," I say and open my legs wider.

"Good girl," he says, and I feel a swell of joy in pleasing him.

He is gentle with me.

Nate pinched and squeezed my little nub roughly, ripping my climax from me. Silas is tender in his attentions, circling my clit with his thick finger over and over again. The tension builds within me, taking me higher until I'm praying he will squeeze it roughly like Nate did so I can rediscover that glorious high.

I'm boneless on the bed at first, but the longer it continues, the more restless I become.

My prayers become vocal. I'm asking him to make it happen.

Then I'm begging for it.

His finger plunging into my drenched channel is shocking. He thrusts in and out several times, and when he touches the little nub again, my body explodes.

I'm boneless again in the aftermath, and the only part of me that moves is my heaving chest as I suck in air. My mind drifts like a leaf in a stream without conscious consideration of a destination. Lying beside me, he arranges my limp body so that it is sprawled over his.

It's the morning, and I should be doing chores, but instead, I'm lying in my bedding nook, wishing he would strip out of the rough clothes so that I might feel his warm flesh again.

The door slamming open stirs me from my semi-doze, and a gust of cold air prickles my skin.

It's Nate, and out the corner of my eye, I see him stacking wood in the storage area beside the fire.

Seeing my study, he winks at me, and a smirk flashes across his handsome face before he turns and leaves again.

My pussy clenches as I remember what he did to me. Discipline should not be an enjoyable experience, and yet submitting to him in this way connects us. While I'm not eager to experience part of it again, what happened afterward was pure joy.

I understand the ways of Alphas and Omegas. But now that they're acting upon me, I'm struck by the strangeness of it—of being *theirs.*

Silas isn't forcing me to sleep again, but despite it being morning, I find myself dozing. The door opens and shuts again, but it doesn't have Nate's signature thud, telling me that this time it's Dax.

I am content.

I don't remember the last time I felt content—perhaps never in this way. My bottom still aches, but it's a distant, buzzing awareness that creates a pleasant stirring between my thighs.

My mind drifts, as it often does, into a world of adventure.

I have a children's book about a princess filled with beautiful illustrations. It's one of my favorites, and I've read it so many times that the pages are fragile and worn. The princess in the picture had blonde hair, while mine is dark red, but I have imagined myself as her many times, and we've enjoyed many adventures.

I press my nose deeper against the safety of Silas's chest as the dream draws me in.

I'm in the forest. Today I'm not wearing my rough brown shirt and trousers, but instead have donned a beautiful gown with flowing royal blue skirts worthy of the princess.

I run—there are distant sounds of battle, and I must hide if I'm to escape capture.

From behind comes the steady thud of pursuit, but the beat is wrong for it to be a man. I lift my skirts and flee as fast as I can. When I glance back, I find I'm being chased by a wolf.

The wolf is enormous—like a horse, fierce and beautiful in the way all deadly animals are. It's a male. I don't know how I comprehend this, but I know that it's true.

Frightened now, my heart is racing, and I know I cannot hope to escape.

The wolf takes me down, tumbling with me, over and over until I am dizzy.

The tumbling stops. I can't see for the hair flying around my face, and can't breathe for the weight pinning me to the ground. The beast is too strong, but I can hear the battle still, and I'm fearful.

Muzzle close to my ear, it growls before its teeth close over the scruff of my neck.

I'm convinced I will be savaged, but all he does is squeeze.

The battle has grown distant, and the pressure of the wolf's teeth instills a sense of calm.

The wolf is not my enemy, I realize; he is my protector.

CHAPTER EIGHT

Nate

The fire is blazing when I leave the cottage after the last of a dozen or so trips. Wood is stacked in the storage alcove inside, and more blocks are stored to the left of the front door. I don't know how long we'll need to stay, but we can't risk moving until she's mated.

It's only been a day, but I'm impatient and hoping that it's soon.

Silas is still with the little Omega in the bedding nook—she is naked, and I've got a feeling she's going to stay that way until she succumbs to her heat.

I wish that I were still in there with her, but Silas is and it's his place and his right. I smirk to myself as I remember her peeking at me from under her lashes as she lay on the bed earlier. Fuck, I want her to misbehave so that I can discipline her again.

The mutt bounds up as I stop in the middle of the courtyard, and I give his head an absent pat. I need a distraction from the beauty lying on the bed. My cock has been semi-hard ever since we arrived at the cottage, and the vision of her naked ass, striped from my belt, consumes my thoughts.

My stomach rumbles, and the mutt whines, reminding me that although the cottage has been stocked with as much food as can be found, it isn't very much.

I'm hungry—I am always hungry. It's part of being a shifter and I have learned to adapt to it. The transition from human to wolf requires a huge amount of energy, and I need to eat a lot.

As I pat the mutt's head, I weigh up my options while staring at the pigpen.

My wolf disdains pig. He would much rather take a deer or rabbit . . . or a plump pheasant or turkey.

There are no such animals within the bounds of the farm, and Silas has forbidden me from shifting and seeking a meal for myself.

I could suffer pig in these circumstances.

My wolf is in agreement. It's pretty much the pig or a few scrawny chickens.

"What do you say, mutt?" His tongue is hanging out, and when I regard him expectantly, he offers a short *woof.* Removing my knife from my belt, I stalk toward the pigpen.

It's dingy and crowded. Why the fuck are there so many full-sized pigs when she was clearly struggling to find food?

Maybe she's not much for killing? That's okay; I eat warm, bloody prey in my wolf form, so it's fair to say I'm not squeamish about much.

Sticking the blade on the top of the post, I wade in to try and grab one.

They don't want to be grabbed.

There is a lot of grunting and squealing long before I can wrestle one out of the pen.

"What the fuck are you doing?" Dax growls. He's been inside the cottage, stacking the last of the wood, so his sudden bellow surprises me.

The pig squeals—I'm still holding it by the ankle, and it's putting up a bastard of a fight.

"What the fuck does it look like I'm doing?" I shout back—I have to shout because the pig senses its imminent demise, and I can't hear myself think over the screeching.

My wolf is not happy with any of this. He doesn't like pig to begin with, but this complete lack of dignity in the face of death erases the little respect he had for the pig.

"Don't kill the fucking pig!" Silas roars, tipping ice into my veins. I only hear that roar when I've really fucked up and he's about to beat me half to death. He's storming toward me, passing Dax, who stands with his hands on his hips.

I'm frightened, but also confused. In one roar, Silas has effectively reminded me who's in charge.

At the cottage doorway, Belle stands, a blanket wrapped around her and her face pale—I don't want to take a beating in front of Belle, but for the life of me, I cannot work out what I've done wrong.

"It's just a fucking pig!" I say, burning with a sense of injustice.

I release the pig.

Still screaming, it bolts off as fast as its fat, stumpy legs will allow, ears flapping and eyes rolling in terror.

I'm certain Silas is about to thump me, but all he does is fist my arm and motion impatiently to Dax. "Get the fucking pig and put it back," he growls to Dax over his shoulder.

I hear Dax cursing. I don't blame him, the pig was a cantankerous bastard before I tussled it around the yard. Now, it has a wild gleam in its beady eyes.

"Go back inside," Silas calls to Belle. She is watching Dax chase the hapless pig around the courtyard.

I'm hauled toward the stable as chaos ensues. "You cannot kill the fucking pigs," Silas mutters once we are well away from the cottage.

"What? Why? Is it diseased?" I pull my arm out of his fist and glare back at Silas.

"She likes the fucking things," he says, swiping a hand through his hair and looking every bit as exasperated as I feel. "I don't claim to understand the nature of her attachment, but she went white as a corpse when she heard it scream—I thought she was going to faint."

"It's a pig," I say, glancing over his shoulder—she's watching Dax chase the pig around the yard. There's a lot of ducking and dodging going on, interspersed by snorting and squealing from the pig and cursing from Dax. "I've never seen a pig that fat. She's been feeding the fucking things more than she's been feeding herself."

"It doesn't matter," he says, then winces—Dax has gotten a hold of the pig, and it's squealing like it's being murdered. "Her heat will never fucking break if we cause her stress now. Just leave the pigs alone."

"There is nothing else but chickens." I thumb in the direction of the coop. "Have you seen the chickens?" I don't wait for him to answer. "Clearly, she doesn't care much about the chickens. They're old and scrawny as fuck. Let me go and hunt. She doesn't have to know how I caught it. I can be discreet."

That earns me a cuff up the side of my head. "You are not fucking discreet! You will bloody it, and come back smeared in the evidence of your prowess. She is not a wolf bitch. She will not be impressed."

He's right, my wolf is not discreet. He's hungry and will probably insist on sampling the carcass before we bring it back. Silas and Dax aren't too picky, but I suspect the little Omega is.

"Fine, the chickens then," I say. All we have are the travel rations, which isn't a problem when I can hunt to supplement the food. I'm desperate for meat and stringy chicken will have to do.

The pig is finally back in its pen, although what we will do with them when we leave is another matter. It's not like we can take them with us.

Dax stalks back to the cottage. He's covered in mud and pauses to strip before dousing himself using a bucket filled from the rainwater tank. Soaking wet, he stomps up the steps naked.

The Omega fled inside after the shirt and before the pants, which is for the best, we don't want to scare her off.

"The chickens," Silas agrees, although he's staring after Dax, probably hoping that the little Omega has thrown herself on the bed and isn't sneaking a look. "Don't bring them in until they are clean and plucked."

He doesn't give me a chance to voice my opinion about plucking a chicken, or how wolves do not *pluck,* since he is already stalking after Dax.

Dax

I am pissed about the fucking pig.

Sometimes I think Nate has lost what little brains he was born with. Maybe it is the nature of being a shifter, all those transitions into an animal can't be good. Perhaps he becomes a little more stupid each time he shifts.

Obviously, she did not want to kill them; otherwise, there wouldn't be nine, fat, healthy-looking pigs milling around in the pen!

Mud splatters my shirt and pants. I only have one clean set left, but these will have to go. I have stripped out of my shirt before I notice the little Omega on the step, watching.

I like her eyes on me, like the little parting of her lips as her gaze travels down. She flees back inside, which is for the best.

I don't want to terrify her unduly before I must.

Stripping the rest of my clothes, I fill a bucket and douse myself. It's fucking freezing, and I can't help but reflect that there is nothing showing to give her cause for concern.

Having rid myself of the filth, I remember that I have taken my pack with the change of clothes inside. A quick glance confirms that Silas and Nate are still having a discussion. The whelp got off lucky with nothing more than a cuff for his dumb pig-wrestling antics—I think the Omega is turning Silas soft.

Sighing heavily, I stomp up the steps and enter the cottage again.

She squeals, which isn't an unusual reaction when a woman sees me naked; however, she isn't even looking at me and has her hand dramatically over her eyes.

I feel a little put out by this. She ogled Nate with slack-jawed interest when he walked in with his shirt off this morning. Last night she slept with Silas while they were both naked so I know she has seen a man before.

Silas slams into the cottage with all the finesse of Nate bringing a gust of sharp wind.

"Put some fucking clothes on," he mutters before ushering Belle to the bedding nook and drawing the curtain closed.

Sighing again, I flip open my pack and rummage for my pants.

"What the fuck is wrong with you," Silas demands in a hushed whisper when he returns to glare at me. "I've seen street whores run screaming. Belle is an untried virgin, I swear you are as thick as Nate sometimes!"

I shove my feet into my pants and pull them up with a scowl. "She didn't see anything—she fled the moment I took my shirt off!" He's definitely turning soft.

"Good," he says, nodding. "She's close."

This peaks my interest, and I forget about the shirt for now. They both put their hands on her, both lay with her in the bedding nook.

They both made her feel good.

All of this is part of the bonding process, and I want my share. Twice, I hauled her back when she was in flight or thinking about it, but those too brief interactions have left me dissatisfied. "I haven't had my time with her," I say gruffly. His eyes narrow—my tone might have come out like a challenge, but I have never been one for subtlety. "I want my turn," I state, not prepared to back down.

His glare is heavy, but it's only fair, and he relents with a nod.

Belle

They're talking on the other side of the room. I can't hear what they are saying, but I suspect it's about me.

I don't want to be in the bedding nook anymore, but Silas put me here and drew the curtain in a way that suggests I shouldn't open it again.

I try peeping through the gap, but Silas has his back to me, and I can't see much. Although I *can* see that Dax has not yet put on his shirt and that produces a strange fluttering low in my belly.

Of the three of them, Dax is the most reserved. He has a gruff, stern way about him that I find intimidating.

It's not only his manner that I find intimidating since he is also a huge, powerful Alpha. My whole body trembles seeing the rippling muscle of his torso and arms that he's hidden beneath his shirt.

They stop talking abruptly, and I jerk back. Footsteps are approaching, and I suffer an irrational urge to flee.

There is nowhere to go. I'm trapped.

The curtain is drawn back—it's Dax. Up close, he appears bigger and more intimidating without the covering of a shirt. I turn away. Every part of me is quaking. Is he about to punish me for spying on them?

"I'm sorry," I say, hoping this will preempt a disciplining.

When I glance up, I find Dax frowning, nostrils flared. "Why? What have you done?"

"I—" Now I have backed myself into a corner, and I've no idea how to respond that will not see them take the belt to my bottom. It's still very sore. I believe it will be painful for the rest of today and for several days to come.

"You are making her nervous," Silas says, pulling out a chair and sitting in such a way that he has a perfect view of the bedding nook.

"Hmm," Dax says—making it clear that he doesn't believe I've done nothing.

Seeing his knee hit the bed, I yelp and turn around.

"I think someone has been up to mischief," he says, thick arm coiling around my waist and bringing me flush to his naked chest.

My body is in a state of riot. The feeling of his warm chest, the thick muscles bunching and sliding where we are pressed together, and his rich Alpha scent are acting upon me like a spell.

"Now," he says, drawing his large hand gently through my hair, brushing it from my hot cheeks. "Tell me what you did to look so guilty."

His tone brokers no argument. My tender bottom is pressing against a thick rod that I'm terrified might be his—

"Uff!" I'm tipped over, and his big hand is now cupping my bottom.

"Don't move," he says gruffly.

Out the corner of my eye, I can see Silas sitting forward in his chair. He's watching this—watching what Dax is doing to me.

Dax is gentle with me. He doesn't pinch the welts like Silas did, but his hand is so big I'm fearful of what he might do.

"You haven't answered," he reminds me. My eyes cut to the left where Silas is sitting—no, he isn't going to help.

My muttered curse earns me a sharp smack to my bottom. "I was trying to hear what you were saying!"

Silas grunts and rolls his eyes. Dax chuckles, and that warm, unexpected noise sets butterflies swirling in my tummy again.

"Rollover," Dax commands.

I do so slowly, reluctant to be exposed to his scrutiny, and yet hopeful that this won't involve a spanking or the belt if my bottom is against the bed.

He cups my chin when I won't look at him, and then I do, and I'm transfixed by his eyes—one is brown, and one is blue-green. I'm still staring at one then the other when his mouth lowers over mine.

The kiss is unexpected—he is the first man to ever kiss me. His lips are warm and silky soft against mine. His rough beard tickles and makes me feel a little hot. He presses firmer, and it seems the most natural thing to let my lips part so his tongue can slide inside.

The kiss robs me of the ability to breathe. My whole body becomes fluttery and flushed like a tide washing over me in never-ending waves. He is so gentle. Yet I sense he's capable of great brutality, and these two determinations go to war. The fear of what such a strong Alpha is capable of reminds me of my weakness.

It reminds me once again that I am prey.

His big, warm hand moves to cup my small breast. He leaves it there, a weight against my chest. My nipple tightens in anticipation, and I become restless.

"Hush," he murmurs against my lips. "Be a good girl for me, and I will make you come."

I can hear the blood rushing through my ears. Twice today, I have come. I shouldn't be greedy, but the mere mention of attention has my pussy drenched.

The hand on my breast moves, squeezing gently before his roughened thumb brushes across my nipple.

"Mmmm!"

My garbled encouragement is swallowed in his kiss. His thumb brushes back and forth slowly, and the bud of my nipple blooms to a hard point.

His head lifts from mine, and I whimper at being denied his mouth.

Then his lips enclose my nipple and half my small breast—and he sucks.

"Oh!" His hand moves to cup my pussy as he sucks gently against my breast. "Oh gods, yes."

I'm cupping his head, delighting in the silken texture of his damp hair, and praying for his fingers to find my swollen bud. My legs fall apart, and my hips rock, trying to encourage his hand to move.

He's not to be rushed, alternating between suckling my breast and licking circles around the engorged tip before pulling as much flesh as will fit into the hot cavern of his mouth.

I am half delirious with need by the time his fingers slip into my slick channel. He pumps a thick finger in and out, making me gasp and grip his hair. The world is moving fast and slow, and I can't focus on all the different sensations engulfing my body.

Then his fingers slide up, catching the sensitive place that feels so good, and I nearly shoot off the bed.

He strums it with his fingertips, side-to-side, over and over, and I'm rushing toward that glorious high.

Then I am falling, and such wild groans pour from my lips that I don't recognize myself.

His lips crash over mine in a hungry kiss as he seduces the last throes of the climax from me.

Abruptly, he rises, and I blink, trying to work out what is happening—it's only then that I hear the growling before Silas takes his place.

He's still fully dressed, and my limp, well-sated body is dragged against his.

I'm sure he is about to finally fuck me, but all he does is press my cheek to his chest where the rumbles are somewhere between a growl and a purr.

I am lost.

I don't know what they are doing to me, but I'm lost.

A force is building on my periphery, and inside me, a pressure rising that I know will soon spillover.

"Sleep, little one," Silas says.

I don't want to sleep, but I'm worn out from my third, shattering climax. My mind is similarly exhausted from the awakening of these strange feelings, and I fall into a fitful doze.

CHAPTER NINE

Silas

I told Dax that he could have his time with Belle, so I should have handled it better. But I'm an Alpha—first Alpha, and although the protection of an Omega necessitates it, sharing is not natural to me.

Once she is settled against me, I relax. I have never spent so much time in bed . . . and with my clothes on. Her heat is close, but I fear our scent alone won't be enough, and we cannot afford to linger here.

Rain begins to patter against the roof, and the room darkens.

The season is changing and the rain will soon turn to snow.

If we don't leave soon, we may be trapped here, and there isn't enough food to last even with nine, overfed pigs. Game is scarcer now and will be more so once winter sets in—there is not enough to support all of us no matter how I try to slice it.

Today is all I can afford to give her; tomorrow, I must force her heat.

This determination does not fill me with joy. My blood is old, and my family highborn. I pride myself on my restraint. Lesser males could not be trusted around her, and we must bond with her so that her scent will change.

Only then will it be safe for us to travel.

I doubt she has ever experienced a heat before, many Omegas do not unless in the presence of an Alpha. Then again, most Omegas don't have an opportunity to grow to maturity like this. Most are taken forcibly, others are bartered for. It takes a powerful family to keep an Omega child safe.

Which is another reason I'm keen for us to return to our family home. I don't like the prospect of traveling with her now—I will like it a lot less if she is pregnant.

The door opens, bringing a gust of icy wind before Dax moves into view.

"Nate's gone scouting," he says. He carries three prepared chickens, which, true to Nate's assessment, are scrawny and barely enough for a meal.

The little Omega's head pops up. "He can't be riding in this weather. What would he even scout for?"

"He's searching for game," I say. It's close enough to the truth. I cannot imagine Oswold will remain in these parts. More likely, he'll find a poor farmer to kill and claim his well-stocked home for the winter.

This thought puts me in a foul mood. It could so easily have been this farm Oswold preyed on. I thank the Goddess herself that it was not, although it doesn't please me to think of another family being subject to Oswold's sick games.

Belle frowns as Dax moves off to light the lamps before preparing to cook the chickens.

"He's not scouting for game," she says, staring straight at me.

For a young Omega who is naked and in the presence of a

dominant male, I find her boldness to be both disconcerting and amusing.

"He'll be back soon," I say. "And if you question me again, I'll take that as an indication you need further discipline."

Her blue eyes turn wary before flashing with heat. "He's not scouting for game, and disciplining me will not change this. Why did you come here? What are three Alpha soldiers of the Imperium Guard doing in the back end of the Empire?"

Dax has stopped what he is doing, although perhaps sensing her censorious gaze has traveled his way, he doesn't turn back.

I don't have the heart to discipline her for her intelligence, although I'd prefer her to remain ignorant of the details.

Her lips start to tremble the longer I don't answer. This little slip of nothing, under the threat of discipline, has backed me into a corner.

"We're tracking criminals," I say.

She makes a bolt out of bed, but I snatch her up before she can get her feet on the floor. "Fetch him back! We can't stay here. It isn't safe."

I pull her into my chest. "We cannot fetch him back. He will return when he is done." She sobs, and it breaks me apart. Her hormones are made volatile by our presence and scent, and although we have yet to mate her, bonds are forming.

She cries although I do not think she fully understands why.

I comfort her as best as I can.

Nate

Upon shifting, I pick up their scent. Given I'm no more than a few miles from the farmstead, this sends my wolf into a spin. I've moved away from the horse to shift, but I can sense its agitation as it picks up on my wolf's mood.

I lope through the dense trees at a brisk pace. It's good to run, the soft, loamy ground beneath my feet is dense with leaves in the turn of the weather. There is a bite to the wind, but it doesn't penetrate my thick coat.

I pause to scent the air. Rain is coming, and there is an icy aspect to it. We are in the farthest northern reaches of the Empire, and winter arrives here first. The smell of fresh pine needles is corrupted by that of unwashed men. I've been the one tracking them whenever the trail dries up, and it is unpleasantly familiar to me.

Loping a circuit, I try to scope out their movement in the area.

Above, clouds gather, ushering in premature darkness.

The fur rises on the back of my neck. They have criss crossed this area many times. I scouted only this morning, but it would seem they've returned . . . and in higher numbers.

The threat they hold to me and mine is palpable. My wolf is going nuts, and I have to force my will upon his to curb his need to attack. It takes a lot to kill a shifter whatever form we choose, but particularly while shifted. But we are far from immortal, and I must be cautious.

As my circles take me closer to the source, I count the individual scents as best as I can. They were no more than six in number last time I picked up their trail, now they are closer to a dozen.

Three or four men, I can take with ease. Six would be a challenge—I cannot take on a dozen, and they're close to Belle's farm.

I'm torn. I should go back and warn my brothers, but I also need to understand the threat's extent.

When I offered to scout this morning, I admit I was reluctant. While I usually wouldn't hesitate to follow up leads on our quarry, I didn't want to leave Belle so close to her heat.

I know they're wondering how I will bond with her—whether I will. She isn't a shifter, and it's unusual for us to mate outside our kind. I have no doubts. From the moment I caught her scent, I'd known it wouldn't matter.

Nose to the air, I draw closer to the freshest source of their trail.

It's not a camp, but they have dismounted in a small clearing where they are engaged in a discussion. My wolf doesn't understand language the way I can in human form. It is too great a risk to shift here, so all I have is the timbre of their voices and their body language to go on.

There is heat to the conversation. I can identify several of Oswold's posse along with others I have not seen before.

I cannot see Oswold.

The hairs on the back of my neck stand to attention again, and I temper the urge to growl.

He isn't here.

Where is he?

The premonition of danger is all-encompassing. The threat is real and present. I must return to the farm where I can warn and protect them.

I spin and take off for the cottage. My paws move so fast they fly over the forest floor as I push myself to my limit. Rain begins to fall, the sky darkens further, and my breath mists the air as I leap over fallen trees and navigate dips and raises of the undulating landscape.

I don't stop to shift but race straight for the little farm.

Danger beats at my psyche.

In my wolf form, there are no gray areas, and decisions are pictured in black or white. Belle is in danger. She is an unmated Omega. Her scent is enough to send lesser Alphas straight into a rut. I do not understand where we might hide nor how we might combat a threat so significant. These are details a wolf is not troubled with; for him, there is only a need to protect at any cost.

Through the trees, I see the shadows of the farm buildings under the dense cover of clouds.

Other shadows are closing in, a movement that signifies men. The glint of metal solidifies into weapons as the odor of stale sweat and liquor taints the cool breeze.

A snarl tears from my open jaws as I leap for the first shape.

He crashes to the ground under my powerful assault, and my jaws close over his throat.

I shake.

It is a glorious moment when I hear the snap as the screaming male loses his grasp on life. His blood fills my mouth and a haze fills my feral mind.

The door to the cottage opens, and my brothers spill out. Around me is the clang of meeting weapons and the cries of men at war.

I leap for the next man, and we roll, a tumbling blur of man and beast. His sword is coming for me, but I take his wrist in a savage bite, snarling as I shake. I am the harbinger of death, and I will destroy every threat.

But I'm sinking further into my wolf, and the man no longer sees the new dangers coming for our door.

Silas

Lamps have been lit, and the fire is blazing.

Nate is still out.

There is a strange premonition growing inside me that all is not right. When he picked up the trail close to the farm this morning, I should have allowed him to follow up on the threat.

Were it not for Belle, I would have.

We are strong men, all of us Alphas, but our greatest strength lies in how we work together. I do not like that he scouts alone. Even when we ride and he takes his wolf form, he is in regular contact.

We have compromised what makes us strong.

A cry from beyond the door rouses us all.

It is a distinct cry, and it is followed by a savage growl.

Nate.

Sword in hand, Dax hastens for the door.

Thudding comes from above. They are on the roof either to block the chimney or to throw something down. I dowse the fire with water just as the room begins to fill with smoke.

Taking up my sword, I point to Belle. "Stay hidden as best you can. If they enter, scream—I will return." She nods swiftly.

It is a terrible thing to see such a fearful expression on a young woman's face. I would stay with her if I could, but our numbers are too small for one of us to sit this out. The back window shutters were boarded and nailed shut by Dax this morning in case our wayward Omega should reconsider escape. The gap is small—she could barely fit through it so I cannot imagine one of Oswold's brigade entering, but I hear the distinct sounds of someone taking an ax to it.

It seems they'll try.

I can't stay with her. We are trapped here, and I must do what I can.

"Bolt the door behind me, and stay hidden," I repeat.

Flinging open the cottage door, I step out.

There are too many, and our chances are not good. This is my first and most pervasive thought as I wade into the fighting.

My sword clashes against a sword, and I thrust against the locked weapons sending the man staggering back before my blade finds a weakness.

He falls, screaming, and I move on to the next. Nate is in his wolf form, his fur up and eyes glazed with rabid fury. His snarls soothe me—they represent exactly how I feel.

The three of us move as one team, protecting each other as we carve and rip our way through those who would attack us. There is an edge to all of us, an extra fierceness and purpose. We have an

Omega to protect, and no one shall pass.

We fight. And although I cannot see where the end is, I sense we are turning the tide. Bodies litter the ground; those who are left are reluctant to come forward.

I no longer wonder if we have a chance, now I know that we do.

Then a scream pierces the air, and all eyes turn toward the cottage. I take a single step before the door is flung open. A young lad has a fist full of Belle's hair and blade against her throat.

My mind grapples for an out.

A thin rivulet of blood spills down her slender throat. Nate growls, but it turns to a whimper as I put a hand to his back.

More men round the corner, among them, Oswold. A twisting knot forms in my gut, and a cold sweat sweeps my spine seeing crossbows aimed our way.

I am dead inside. We have all failed her, but I am first Alpha and I have failed her the most.

Dax tosses his sword to the floor.

There is nothing.

We have nothing.

The air shifts, and where a wolf once was, Nate stands, chest heaving from the fight and body glistening with sweat.

We have nothing.

I toss my sword to the ground besides Dax's and our enemy swarms to restrain us.

They have plans for us that do not only involve our death.

And that means we have something.

CHAPTER TEN

Belle

I am prey.

This is not pity talking; this is an acknowledgment of a fact. I am small and weak; I am an Omega. I am a prize that men war over.

For a year, I have hidden in this distant corner of the Empire.

But my time of hiding is over, and I find myself amid such a war.

For tonight has brought strangers to my door who remind me that I am prey.

Immediately, I understand the difference between the two parties of men. Silas, Dax, and Nate are honorable soldiers like my father. These newcomers are dirty, unwashed outlaws who smell strongly of liquor. They wear the same Imperium uniform, but it is torn and tattered and commands no respect.

They have no respect, not for me, not for life, and not for the symbol of our Empire. They will use me for their lust until there is nothing left of me.

A faint shimmering of the air and Nate is standing where the wolf was.

A shifter.

I have seen lesser shifters but have never seen a wolf. My father said they keep to their own kind mostly, and that Silas called Nate 'brother' confuses me.

But there is no time to explore the otherworldly beauty he possesses in each form. There is a blade against my throat. I feel the sting where it has nicked my skin and the sticky trickle of blood smearing my skin.

Crossbows are pointed at my three Alphas, and our enemy is many in number—we don't have a chance.

With barked orders, we are taken back into the house. Dax fights when they take him. It takes four of them to beat him to the ground. I feel every blow like it is against my own flesh. Every savage punch and kick breaks another piece of my soul. When they are done, he hangs limp between them as they drag him into my little home.

It is cold and dark within—the fire out after Silas doused it. I have let them down. I didn't scream loud enough . . . I didn't fight hard enough when the young ruffian climbed through the window and put a knife to my throat.

I'm thrust inside where I find myself surrounded by a jeering wall of stinking male flesh. I fear they are about to rut me, but the scarred one whom I take for a leader takes his sword to his own men in a violent, bloody thrust. "Mine!"

The remainder retreat warily. My breathing is a shallow pant. Hot blood coats my naked body, and I'm shaking up a storm.

As the leader turns a slow circle, silence falls.

Then he smirks and sheaths his sword, and with an impatient gesture to the young man holding me, I'm drawn from the crowd. I'm forgotten for the moment as lamps are lit, and they bring supplies and liquor into the tiny cottage, crowding it with their raucous presence. The dead lumps of flesh are carried out as if they are of no importance. They care nothing for their own brothers' lives.

They are callous.

And their souls are dark as night.

Dax is unconscious, and seeing the man who was so gentle with me earlier in the day lie lifeless, is harrowing.

My breathing is choppy but turns erratic as they make new entertainment with Silas. It is a terrible thing to witness, human cruelty. I have read of adventures and battles with brave heroes and heroines, and I understand that war and warring is a vicious business.

But as I watch this unfold, as I see the blood splatter and hear the grunt as they take their vengeance upon Silas, I am stirred by a dark, hopeless rage.

I understand what this is about. The three Alphas have dared to fight back, and in doing so, killed many of their men. They will have their sport first with my men and then with me.

Silas is a swaying lump of raw flesh. I will not turn away from what they do, although his eyes implore me to. How he takes so much is beyond my comprehension. My heart wants to give out from the pressure, it beats so wildly in my chest.

It goes on forever, trapping me in this desperate dreamscape.

Silas endures. It makes what they did to Dax look like play, and still, he endures.

Finally, when he is retching on his knees, they move on to Nate. The young bandit has forgotten me caught as he is in the fervor of this abuse.

Our captors delighted in Silas and Dax's attempts to fight back, but Nate is bound with hands behind his back, on his knees, naked.

The scarred leader has a glint in his eyes as he takes out a knife. He spits in Nate's face and plays in it with the tip of his blade. Blood springs out a light trickle that turns into a gush.

"Shifter scum," the man grits out. "Raping our women folk with your dog cock. Filthy animals."

There is nothing filthy or animalistic about Nate—it's almost as if this heinous man is describing himself. I didn't turn away from what they did to Silas, but the knife carving into Nate's beautiful face is a new level of horror.

"Come on, wolf-boy," the man taunts. He fists Nate's head to hold him still. The others cheer and offer encouragement to their leader to 'cut him deeper' and 'make him pay'.

I am repulsed. Nate is shaking violently as the knife presses ever deeper, drawing sickening patterns in his flesh.

Tears spill down my cheeks. I am forgotten as they become riveted by the bloodletting, and they are hungry for more.

This is impossible. It is hopeless.

Nate continues to shake violently, his body racked by pain and an otherworldly force.

Then it happens, a ripping of the fabric of the universe, and his face contorts into a wolf's head before morphing back again.

A sickening cheer goes up. They hoot and holler, "Again!"

He cannot shift fully with the rope binding his hands. His face is once more perfect when he shifts back with an inhuman roar. The man holding him laughs as he goes back to his dark work.

And so the next level of torture begins.

I pray to the Goddess as I witness Nate's ruination. The men are crowded around me, jeering and taunting. They are calling him an animal, but it is they who are nothing more than beasts. Each time he shifts, my heart surges with the hope that he might finally break free.

He does not.

He is a beautiful predator, and they are determined to break him.

I have done this to them. Were it not for me, they would never have put down their weapons and submitted. They would have died fighting.

I would rather die fighting.

There is no risk that I would not take to escape this cycle of despair. The time between his shifts grows longer—this is costing him, and he cannot keep doing this.

Eventually, he will not be able to shift.

My eyes skitter over the occupants of the room before meeting those of Silas. There is so much pain there. He is willing me to look away.

I cannot.

As I turn back to Nate, I notice the small knife left upon the table.

It is meant for cutting meat or bread. It is not sharp like the blade cutting into Nate's flesh.

But it is a knife.

My eyes dart back to Silas. He knows what I was looking at, and there is a warning in his eyes. These monstrous men are not paying attention to me yet—but soon they will, and this opportunity will be over.

The slight tightening of his jaw tells me Silas knows what I am about. There is no blade at my throat now. There is nothing to stop them from fighting. I would rather fight than this. Dax is conscious again, and something in the way I am staring at Silas has alerted him, and he shifts slowly to his feet.

The jeering men do not notice, but Nate is nearing his limit, and I don't like to consider what will happen then to him or me.

I need a distraction.

Silas shakes his head.

My jaw tilts in defiance.

I am small and weak. No one fears me.

But I'm also brave and fearless, and I will not go to these men without a fight.

They are merciless and unworthy of an Omega. When they have finished debasing my Alphas, they will abuse and rut me until I am broken, perhaps until I am dead.

I'm terrified, but I will take any risk to make this nightmare end.

Silas sees all this in my face.

Outside I may be small and weak, but inside I have the soul of a warrior goddess.

Nate is cut to pieces and panting hard. I must act now before it is too late.

Silas roars, and lowering his head charges the nearest man. A cry goes up as the men rush to try and beat him down, but I don't allow myself to dwell on that.

They're distracted.

The blunt knife is in my hand, and I'm sawing at Nate's ties.

"What the fuck are you doing?" Nate growls under his breath.

What I'm doing should be obvious, but perhaps all the shifting has addled his mind. "I'm saving you so that you can save me," I hiss back. The room has descended into pandemonium.

Everything is slow and fast, and my world is coming through a tunnel so narrow that I can barely see.

Then the rope springs free. "Hide," Nate growls.

Then he is gone, and where Nate once lay stands a vicious snarling wolf.

He is huge.

He is terrifying.

He is a beast.

And he is death.

He is a nightmare that they have been toying with, and he will have his revenge.

I cower under the table as the screams and snarls engulf my tiny cottage. Blood splatters and men fall, but they are not my men falling, and I welcome every death.

The cacophony gives way to a silence that is broken by ragged breathing. The door has been opened during the fray, and frigid air whistles through the cottage.

My ears are ringing, and I lift my lashes slowly.

The wolf stands in the middle of the room. He is bloody and wounded as he pads over to me and licks my face once before collapsing with his head upon my lap.

I sob as I pet his beautiful face. "No, Nate. No!"

He is breathing. I can hear the raspy pant, but it is weak. He cannot be about to die; I won't allow it!

Silas crouches before the table where we are. His face is a swollen mess, but he seems more alert than Nate. Beyond him, Dax watches—he's in no better shape.

They are both capable of standing, and that is far more than Nate.

He puts a hand on Nate's side and gives it a gentle pat. "Shift back. You are frightening her. She thinks you're about to die."

The wolf whines. He is in terrible pain, I know he is.

Then the air shifts like a crackling of space and time, and Nate is lying there.

I wail and throw my arms around him.

Today, I have learned that I am brave—that the heart of a warrior goddess beats inside me.

But I am also small and weak, and the world is very cruel. I need strong mates who can protect me and the children I will bear them.

In so short a time they have impressed themselves upon me deeply. There is equality in this, and in joining, we each bring a worthy part that makes a perfect whole.

I want my heat to come and be part of them, but I recognize that it will not be tonight.

We are alive, the nightmare is over, and I'm grateful for that.

Silas

Nate untangles himself with a pain-filled hiss that I feel to my core. I coax Belle out of her hiding place and press her cheek to my chest. It's bloody, but I need her to take in my scent and to find calm after what has been done in this tiny cottage.

A still-naked Nate stumbles off to help Dax toss the bodies outside while our little one clings to me. Her home is destroyed, but it seems of little consequence now. A few of them have fled—Oswold among them. But he will not be back tonight.

"I want Nate." She is shaking, but there is defiance in her tone.

Nate is carrying the legs of one of Oswold's thugs, Dax holds the arms. Their heads swing around. They are as shocked as I am by her outburst. Nate is half-wolf, and those less familiar with shifters fear his kind. But he is part of us, and she has watched him being tortured.

I had doubts that he would bond with her, but now I have none. He awaits my response, since I am first Alpha, but there is desperate hopefulness in his eyes. There's no mark or blood on him, but his face has the drawn look it gets if he shifts too many times. He needs to eat . . . now I sound like a parent! But he is the youngest of us, and at times I forget how young.

Dax grunts and Nate turns back to face him—they lob the body through the open door before returning their attention to me.

I may be first Alpha, but we each have strengths. Tonight I saw a side of Nate that I have never seen before. It is the Omega acting upon him—she is acting upon us all, making us more than we were.

I nod "Don't—"

"I won't," he says.

"Draw the curtain," I add.

He swipes a hand through his tangled hair and offers up a tired grin.

Giving her over to his care is harder than I thought possible.

There is a stretched moment where I hold her slight body tighter than I should before I force my fingers to relax. The need to scrutinize her for harm is as strong as my urge to take her to the bloody floor and rut her. I cannot allow myself to dwell upon what nearly came to pass—we could have lost her tonight. She is a brave little warrior Omega, and we are Goddess-blessed to have her.

"Check her throat," I say gruffly. No sooner do I step back than Nate has swept her into his arms and is stalking toward the bedding nook.

I catch Dax's grin when I turn back. "His ego is already the size of the Empire," he says with a roll of his eyes.

I bark a laugh. The blood lust is heavy upon me, but Dax's dry humor lessens the weight. I help him gather the next partially-dismembered body, and we toss it out the door. It takes us a good while to straighten the cottage as best as we can. We are exhausted by the time it's done.

Dax lights the fire.

As I glance at the bed, I see Nate and our Omega are already fast asleep, their bodies pressed tightly together.

Love, fierce and deep crashes over me. There was a dark moment tonight when I feared I would watch them suffer and die before I met a similar end. I know the way Oswold's mind works. The sick bastard likes to play with his victims.

"He did good," Dax says gruffly. His face is contorted with swelling and cuts, but his Alpha genes will see him heal swiftly. It has been many months since I saw my own face in a mirror, but I expect I look much the same.

"I will take first watch," I say. "Tomorrow, I'll have Nate scout, and we can better assess the remaining threat."

He nods. "I doubt I'll get much sleep." Then he gestures toward the sleeping pair. "He's going to have to eat the horse tomorrow if she won't let us kill the fucking pigs." And with that parting grouch, he goes and lays down on his bedroll with a pained grunt.

Taking up my sword, I go outside, circling the home and listening for any sign of trouble. It is here that I discover Shep. Standing over him is Nate's horse, still wearing his tack and saddle.

The horse doesn't worry me—Shep does. He lays on his side, breathing shallowly with a vicious gash to his hind leg. He tries to stand as I approach. "Down," I growl. The dumb fucking dog will open the wound worse.

He whines, and his tail thumps the floor as he tries to scramble closer. Crouching beside him, I still him with my hand. "Be still, mutt." A chunk of his ear is missing, and he is covered in cuts and scrapes, but the gash is deep, and I don't think he will survive.

It would be a kindness to put him out of his pain, and I reach for the knife tucked at my belt.

He whines again, tail still thumping and sad eyes staring up at me through the gloom.

"Fuck," I mutter as I put the blade away. He whimpers as I lift him up and carry him over to the barn. The horse follows us into the shelter, finding a nearby bale of hay and nipping at it with half-hearted interest.

Returning to the cottage, I collect a lamp and supplies. Despite his determination that he wouldn't sleep, Dax is out cold.

Back in the barn, I stitch the mutt up as best I can. He's lost a lot of blood, and his chances aren't good. It would be kinder to end his suffering, but I know our little Omega would want me to try.

So I try.

A makeshift bandage around his body and an old horse blanket for comfort, I leave him inside a stall in case the dumb beast tries to follow me.

I go and see to Nate's horse next, before making a circuit of the perimeter.

There is no sign of Oswold.

Exhausted from the fight, and drained from what has followed, I struggle to stay awake.

I pace. I check on the mutt, who is no better or worse, and pace some more.

Finally, as dawn creeps over the farmstead, a butt-naked Nate staggers out of the cottage. "I need to get my horse," he says as he sees me approaching.

I thumb in the direction of the stable.

"Good, then I need to eat. Don't try and stop me from hunting. I'm hungry enough to gnaw my own arm off. I hunt or I eat a fucking pig."

"You can hunt," I say. I'm about to ask him if he's well enough, but he has already shifted and is bounding off.

An hour later, Nate returns dragging a half-eaten deer carcass between his teeth. He drops it at my feet and shifts. Smirking, he pats his protruding belly. "I needed that. No sign of them," he adds. His smile drops. "I have a feeling we've not seen the last of Oswold."

I'm worried that he's right.

CHAPTER ELEVEN

Dax

The tiny Omega is inspecting me, and I'm not happy about this.

I lie. I'm happy to have her hands upon me, but I'm not pleased with the implication that I need coddling.

"Does it hurt very much?" she asks.

I shake my head. It hurts like a bastard but I would never admit as much.

She has sat me on the bench before the wide oaken table. Here, she's leaning over me, her fingers gentle in my hair as she brushes it back so she can see the cut on my temple. The position places her small tits level with my eyes, and I remember how the needy tips grew taut when I sucked on them yesterday.

She has put a dress on, which is both a disappointment and a relief. My dick is stone hard, and I swear I will throw her down on the table and mount her if she doesn't move away soon.

The door is thrust open before I can succumb to my basal urge.

A gust of cold wind accompanies the arrival of Silas.

His eyes narrow like he knows all the dark thoughts consuming me. It isn't hard to guess, there is a telling bulge in my pants, and her tits are inches from my face.

"Help Nate with the deer," he barks. Stalking over, he snatches her away. He has her in the bedding nook a moment later, turning her face so he can study the small cut on her throat. It angers me to see her flesh marred by even a minuscule cut like that—I already checked it myself before I allowed her to fuss over me.

I suck in a deep breath and will the blood to give up the stranglehold it has on my cock. It doesn't help that her scent is rich in the confined space.

"I need to taste you, Belle," Silas mumbles. "I promise it will make you feel good—I need this."

Fuck! I should be leaving; he's ordered me to leave. But the sight of her on her back in the bedding nook, dress thrust up and legs spread wide as he buries his head between them robs me of thought and breath.

"Oh!" Her breathy moan snaps me back. My fucking dick will never go down! He yanks her bodice down and palms her tits as he eats her out. Her scent is so thick in the air I fear I may pass out.

Somehow, I get to my feet and stumble for the door. It slams behind me as I exit, and I lean against it breathing deeply.

The tension is escalating. Her heat will break soon, I know this. The events of last night have our lust rising even higher.

The bodies are gone, and the foul scent of burning flesh wafts on the chill air.

A half-eaten deer lies in the middle of the cobbled courtyard . . . I can only presume Nate has been allowed to hunt.

Much of it is missing.

Maybe the mutt has also been at it?

I've gotten used to Nate chewing on his kill before he brings it back when he is particularly hungry, but my lips curl in disgust at sharing it with the mutt.

My dick has softened, which is a small positive consideration.

I hear mumbled talk coming from the barn, and I stalk over, determined to get to the bottom of what happened to the deer.

"You're going to be okay, boy," Nate is saying. "If you don't try and fucking move." He's on his knees beside the mutt, feeding him slivers of venison. He's naked. But like all shifters, he doesn't feel the cold.

The mutt's tail thumps against the floor, but the fact he has to be coaxed to eat tells me he's not well.

"What happened?" I ask.

Nate glances over his shoulder and, seeing me, slowly stands. As he turns, I can see his distended abdomen. I'm surprised he hasn't made himself ill gorging like that.

"One of Oswold's bastards cut him. Silas found him last night. He's eaten a little, so that is a good sign." He nudges his head toward the door. "Is she okay?"

I grimace. "She was until Silas buried his head between her thighs."

Nate frowns and rubs absently at his belly. "She doesn't enjoy it?"

"Of course she fucking enjoys it," I snap, wondering at my restraint in not thumping him up the side of the head. "I swear you are as dense as the damn mutt sometimes."

The mutt, knowing we are talking about him, whines and his tail thumps against the ground.

Nate belches loudly. "Good—her heat will break soon. Help me with the deer."

Silas

I have been feasting on the Omega for what feels like hours, gluttonous for her taste. My face is numb, and she is a limp, insensible puddle on the bed by the time I finally lift my head. Her parted thighs glisten with her slick, and her small tits are red where I have mauled them.

Swaying a little as I gain my feet, I swipe a hand over my face. Belle's scent is all over me, and I'm teetering on the brink of my rut. My iron will alone holds me back from falling upon her like a savage. The arrival of her heat is a battle of wills between her and me, and I will win if it fucking kills me.

I fear it will kill me.

I am trying to force her heat in the gentlest way I can. Delusional, I know, there *is* no gentle way.

The door slams open. It's Nate; he will never change. "Shep is looking better," he says. There are two legs of venison over his shoulder . . . and I notice his stomach has returned to normal.

Also, he's naked.

"Shep?" Her head pops up. I swear she was asleep a moment ago.

I cut a scowl at Nate—he shrugs. "Put your fucking clothes on," I mutter before turning back to the tiny Omega I have so recently ravished upon the bed. Buttoning her dress, she scrambles from the bed.

"What happened to Shep?" There is a high, anxious quality to her voice.

I cuff Nate. He grunts but otherwise appears unconcerned. If my knuckles weren't still sore and swollen, I would bloody the whelp's nose.

I snag Belle around the waist before she can bolt for the door. "Shoes!"

Muttering under her breath, she goes and puts them on . . . but doesn't stop to fasten them before darting outside.

"She'll break her damn neck," I growl as I stalk after her.

As I reach the doorway, I see her disappearing into the barn. Dax is standing in the entrance with a forlorn expression on his face. He doesn't do emotions. She's attached to the fucking pigs, I can't imagine how she must be seeing the injured mutt.

I stalk over to the barn where I find her on her knees, sobbing over Shep. The damn beast is lapping the attention up, tail thumping the floor in double time.

"He's fine," I say, feeling as awkward as Dax looks. I don't actually know if this is true, but if his tail is any indication, he is definitely feeling better.

"He is not fine! Oh, what did they do to your beautiful ear!"

Beautiful is a charitable term to be applied to the beast's ear with or without the missing chunk . . . and it is the least of Shep's concerns.

"He is stuffed full with prime venison," Dax grumbles. "If he dies, he'll die happy."

We both wince when she begins to wail.

"He's putting on a show for sympathy," Nate says. "All warriors have battle scars."

I was so preoccupied with the broken Omega on her knees that I didn't notice his approach. He has put his pants on but his feet and chest are still bare.

Crouching beside her, he puts a hand on the mutt's shoulder. "Good boy, Shep. Let's show Belle how you can stand. He took a blade. I've given him a little devil root to keep him sleepy. He can stand, but I don't want him running around for a few days."

As Nate lifts the horse blanket, Shep gains his bandy feet, and Belle cries anew as she throws her arms around his neck.

I'm trying to decide if this new development is positive when I notice that she has not fastened the buttons on her dress properly, and I'm distracted by the vision of her small tits nearly spilling out as she pets the excited mutt.

Dax makes a choking sound—I suspect he's also staring at her tits—and stomps off back to the cottage.

It takes us a good while to encourage her to leave Shep so he can rest. I let Nate do the talking. He's more patient than I. Finally, we return to the cottage.

The remainder of the fruit stores have been brought in, and the room is filled with the scent of roast venison—a marked difference from yesterday evening when we were fighting for our lives.

"Oh!"

Her exclamation accompanies me divesting her of the dress. It's warm inside the home, but that isn't the reason I have removed it. I need her in heat, the danger we experienced last night makes it imperative.

She must be claimed.

We cannot afford to wait.

Pulling out a rickety chair, I put her on my lap. Nate leans against the wall near the door, arms folded. Dax takes a bench at the table.

She tries to get down. I growl. It's aggressive, steeped with all the dark, festering emotions I'm feeling when I remember how close we came to losing her.

As she stills, my awareness rises. A prickling sensation washes over my skin, and all my senses scream to alert.

I growl again, and she shudders. She stops fighting, and her face presses close to my chest, where an Alpha's scent is most potent.

A growl, long and low, rumbles in my chest.

"Oh," she says. Her small hands, which were fisted against my chest, suddenly lower to press against her belly. "No!"

I see her stomach ripple under her hands as a contraction grips her womb.

Heat.

My heart rate jacks up, and my dick thuds heavily against her hip as I prize her small hands away so I can better see what's happening.

Her cry is one of torment as her stomach muscles contract.

Heat.

"It's okay, little one. Your body is preparing for an Alpha—this is natural." I hold her still, pinning her hands at the small of her back, the other holding her knees down when she tries to draw them up.

Heat.

This is painful for her, I understand this, and hate how it hurts her.

But the Alpha in me is aroused and rejoicing. As the air thickens with her potent pheromones, I sense my brothers awakening to her change.

I've been holding myself—and my rut—by a thread.

She throws her head back and screams, but all I hear is the snapping of the thread.

CHAPTER TWELVE

Belle

I'm on the beast's lap, naked, and the subject of violent cramping. I want to curl up into a ball and hide from this misery, but he has me trapped and open, and I can only endure.

"Breathe deeply for me, nice big breaths, and it will be over," he says, his voice a low rumble close to my ear. "Good girl."

Instinctively, I obey, sucking in great gulps of air even though it makes the cramping worse. I'm panting and crying again. I feel as though I'm about to die.

Pressure is building inside me and bearing upon me from all sides. I feel sick and a little woozy—high, like I've eaten too many moon berries.

He places his big hand so that it is splayed over my stomach. Soothing back and forth over the rippling, tormented muscles.

The pressure is a living entity that lifts me ever higher.

I'm feverish. Silas's scent is inside me, setting my skin on fire.

Then it bursts. A place deep inside my womb bursts and hot,

sticky fluid gushes from between my legs.

"Oh!" I wail and thrash against his hold. He growls. The sound is sharp and feral, and I instantly still. I'm sobbing, chest heaving, and mortified by the puddle I've made across his lap. The absence of the terrible pressure leaves me wrung out. In place of the pressure, there is a growing sense of heat.

"Open," he commands.

I don't understand—then he taps my thigh, and I do.

"Open for me, Belle."

There is compulsion laced in his voice, and the desire to obey is strong. But I'm embarrassed by what has happened.

Tightening his hold on my wrists, he forces my back to arch, pushing my breasts up.

I need to obey. I *should* obey. But I don't want to—I'm not ready to yet.

The knuckles of his free hand brush over my left breast. "Open," he growls.

This time it is more than a compulsion, it is an imperative, and I jerk my thighs apart.

"Good girl."

His lips brush against my hair as his knuckles skim back and forth across my breast driving the sensitive nipple to a hard peak. I feel tiny beside him. They're all big, powerful men, and they are completely overwhelming me.

Then Silas squeezes my nipple—hard.

I gasp and clamp my legs shut.

He growls and twists my nipple, gentling the touch when I open for him again.

I don't understand what he's doing to me or my reactions. When Dax put his mouth there, he was gentle. Silas isn't, he is rough with them, even rougher than he was earlier when he licked and sucked the hard nub between my legs.

I'm hot, and inside, the contractions start again. This time they're different, deeper, lower, they're in my pussy, like a low-burn climax simmering under the surface. He torments my nipples with lazy cruelty. My body throbs in an echo of each squeeze and twist, pulsing the sticky slickness out.

I am—empty. I need something, but I don't understand what.

He shifts attention to my neglected breast, and for reasons I cannot explain, this drives the heavy, pulsing sensations higher still.

"Gods, please!" He isn't a god, not mine, not anyone's, but I beg him like he might be one.

My thighs have opened wider. I become aware of Dax and Nate watching, their eyes locked on the damp flesh that Silas has forced me to expose.

Lust darkens their faces. I haven't thought about man's basal side often, being closeted from it all my life. Today, as I suffer sweet torment from a man who is both my captor and protector, I'm being educated as to its nature.

"What do you need?" Silas demands.

He's asking me like I have the answer. I don't have the answer. I'm convinced that *he* is the one with the only answer to be had.

"Answer me," he growls, giving my nipple a sharp twist and tug that has me squirming, gasping, and moaning on his lap.

"I don't know!"

He lets off his pinching and slaps my breast.

The sting is sharp and sends it jiggling before he pinches my nipple again.

Heat blooms all over my skin, and my pussy aches in a way that demands to be filled.

"I need you. I'm so empty. Please!"

Silas

All Alphas can read an Omega; our basal instincts guide us.

She is ready. Seeing her young body prepare itself for us, watching her enter her heat, and hearing the soft moans as I toy with her sweet body, is pure joy.

I don't know what fate should deliver such a treasure to us as a mate, but I'm determined our first coupling will be everything she needs.

And she needs to be dominated.

I sense Dax and Nate's rapt interest. The scent of her slick permeates the air. Her legs are open wide, and her hips wriggle encouragement for me to move my attention there.

She gasps at the first pass of my fingers through the slick folds. A pretty flush has spread from her cheeks down to the swell of her small breasts. Her nipples, after my attention, are rosy-red and beautifully distended. Pulling her back flush to my chest, I widen my legs so that she is splayed open before my brothers as I spear my fingers into her weeping cunt.

Her back arches and a breathy moan escapes her parted lips as her small hands clamp over my wrists. I pinch and twist her nipple as I plunge my fingers in and out.

She is tight.

Two of my thick fingers present a challenge, and it takes several minutes to work them both fully in. Belle gasps and cries and tries to ride my fingers.

She's in heat, and she needs to be filled. But her young, untried body is slow to catch up.

Her rich pheromones are intoxicating, and Nate and Dax have moved closer.

Mouth open, she chants little prayers as I curve my fingers inside her and find the sweet spot to encourage her to open up. As she begins to loosen around my thrusting fingers, I force the third one in, working her without mercy.

Stretching her.

Each penetration goes a little deeper. Wet slapping sounds permeate the air. She may be tight, but her body is copious with slick, and that will make it easier when I fill her with my cock.

"Please, please, please."

Her begging brings a stony hardness to my cock. Earlier, when I had her on her back as I feasted on her pussy, I brought her to climax over and over again. But I don't want her to come yet, or she will tighten, and I will never get inside. I slow my movements, then hold still and scissor my fingers until I can force them deeper inside.

I hold her body immobile, forcing her to endure the fullness, growling in her ear to encourage more slick to spill. She clenches, pulsing slick over my fingers.

"Please, Silas."

She's sobbing with frustration, but I'm sinking into my rut and don't allow it to deter me from what must be done. Outwardly, I'm cold and detached as I torment her body. Inside, I am burning hot as I anticipate forcing her open and breaching her virgin cunt.

"What is happening to me?" Her voice is a needy whimper.

"You're going into heat, little one. Your body is preparing for what must be done. We will rut you—it is what you need."

Stretching my fingers, I sink deeper, feeling for the barrier. When I meet it, she squeals and tries to wrest my hand away. It is thick and rubbery and resistant when I test it.

At my soft, rumbling purr, her body loosens and she submits to my exploration with only the occasional whimper or hiss of complaint. "Let me do this, Belle."

I play with her, enjoying the building anticipation, letting it rise until it reaches desperation.

Reluctantly, I ease my fingers from her.

It is time.

Belle

I am naked and needy, the heady combination of their three scents working as a potent aphrodisiac. I can't think anymore; I'm an animal with needs. The sensation of Silas's fingers deep inside has driven me into a frenzy.

Standing, Silas carries me to the bed where he drops me onto the rumpled bedding.

"Don't touch," Silas says, voice stern and dark eyes flashing in the firelight.

Simultaneously I want to touch and not-touch. He has size and power, but I don't fear him, and there is an allure to defying his command.

"For fuck sakes, hold her. Little Omega is going to test us all," Silas mutters. His brothers approach. Nate strips his pants off before crawling over to my left, his heavy cock swollen and glistening with pre-cum. He's smirking, but it has a dark edge to it that makes me breathless. He catches my hands before I can grasp his cock and shakes his head in warning.

But I'm distracted because Dax is also stripping. The vision of his massive chest and thick arms robs my lungs of air. Goddess, he is a stunning male.

Unlike Nate, he doesn't strip completely, but I don't have time to wonder because he is climbing onto the other side of me and taking my right hand from Nate.

They each take a hand—pressing them to the soft, fur-covered bedding above my head. I hiss a little complaint as I test their hold.

Heat blooms in my belly. They're close, restraining me, stopping me from playing in the needy place between my legs.

And I like it.

They're purring, they are all purring, and the deep rumbles invade me. My eyelids grow heavy. I'm heavy everywhere like the energy has drained from me.

Through hooded eyes, I watch Silas undress. Piece by piece removing clothing, exposing walls of hard, rippling Alpha male. I have no point of reference, I had never seen a man nude before Silas, Dax, and Nate arrived. His cock juts from a nest of dark hair. It is thick, long, and ruddy red in color, and I have no idea how it will fit.

But I want to try.

He is beautiful. Not in the way of the trees in fall, or the prince in my book.

But in the way of a deadly predator. My stomach turns over thinking about what he has done to me . . . what they have all done to me since we first met so short a time ago.

I don't want his hands or his mouth on me now. I want him inside me.

He takes it in his hand and jacks his fist up and down. Whimpering, I open my legs wider, silently begging him to give me what I need. His nostrils are flared, and his chest heaves as he continues his slow pumping. I lick my lips seeing the clear sticky fluid pooling at the tip. The sight is captivating. He's an animal in its prime—he is a worthy mate.

They all are.

They have shown me many times.

I'm restless. Their deep purring is settling an otherworldly quality to the moment. My legs are open, and I like that Silas is staring at the hot place I have exposed. I want him and his thick cock—crave it, although I know that it will hurt.

My lips are dry, and I feel thirsty, but I don't believe it is water that I need. A primitive force is taking over me.

The cramping begins again, low in my womb, tearing a scream from my lips. I try to curl into a ball, but Nate and Dax take my thighs, dragging me open again. The stickiness is pooling out, drenching the bedding. The pain of the cramping is all-encompassing—I'm on the brink of insanity.

A new, roughened hand makes contact, skimming over my hip and splaying across my rippling stomach. I blink tears away and stare up into Silas's beautiful face. He is over me, crowding me.

And he's purring—it blends with that of Dax and Nate—my body vibrates with it. Fist planted beside my head, he lines up with my entrance. His purr dips to a growl as he thrusts.

I scream. I'm broken. Silas has broken me . . . he has ripped me apart.

A hot, silken rod is buried inside me. It burns and pulses. Tears stream down my cheeks. I beg him to take it out. I am trapped and surrounded.

"Breathe, Belle," Silas growls.

I suck in air—I hadn't realized that I stopped. It brings their rich pheromones deep, and my eyes roll back.

I hiss when he dares to withdraw. His responding growl is utter domination, and he surges deeper again. Goddess help me, there is more. How is it possible for there to be more? I'm speared by his hot burning flesh. I thrash my head from side to side. There are too many conflicted parts to what is happening, and I'm at the apex of the chaos.

He batters at me, each thrust surging a little deeper. There is so much slick but it doesn't seem to help. The cramping is back, and my whole abdomen aches.

Then something snaps, I feel a sharp tug deep inside, and then his abdomen is flush to mine. His huge hand splays over my collarbone, his thumb against my throat. "Breathe Belle," he repeats. "The worst is over now."

Silas

Her hot cunt pulses around my rod. She's tight and the pressure is intense. Held open, she has no choice but to submit.

Her whimpers of pain turn to raw moans of pleasure as I begin to rut her, using her young body the way she needs.

Soon she demands more. Her little growls of displeasure and the way she tries to rock her thoroughly-trapped hips to meet my thrusts tells me she has succumbed to her heat.

And we have barely begun.

"Open your eyes," I growl when she closes them. I pinch her cheeks roughly until her lashes crack to slits. Mumbled nonsense that doesn't hint at words spills from her lips as our eyes lock. Our bodies slap together amid the glorious, feral sounds of our rutting. Dax and Nate have released her long since, and although they remain close, my little Omega prey consumes all my attention.

She may be ours, but she is mine first.

"Come for me, Belle. Come for your mate."

Her glazed eyes never leave mine as her body splinters under me. Her mouth opens on a silent scream that erupts into wild pleasure as she spasms around me. My thrusts slow, and I push deeper, feeling the swelling grow until it locks us together and my balls tighten.

My brain shuts down as hot jets of cum spill out.

Growling my satisfaction, I fist her hair as I bite over the juncture of her shoulder and throat.

Blood pools in my mouth, and she screams again, her pussy fisting me and drawing more of my seed.

In the moments following, I come to understand a future I had never dared to consider. Omegas are rare, highly sought, and I never expected one to be mine.

She is not *only* mine, I remind myself. She belongs to all of us . . . and another should Bram be man enough to yield.

My eldest brother is a distant consideration. The Omega is barely conscious when my knot eases enough to escape her hot cunt.

Nate will have her next. This is nothing to do with our hierarchy. Dax is hung like a bull, and it's only fair that Nate gets to enjoy the tightness of her sheath before Dax utterly ruins it. Not that Nate is lacking . . . and there is still her ass to enjoy once we have bred her.

I can say with confidence that Dax is never getting that tree stump in her ass.

There is no need for words, and my jaw tightens as Nate takes my place. It is one thing to fuck a woman and another to see your brother do the same.

There's no preamble. Flipping her onto her stomach, he takes her hips in his hands, dragging her soft, well-fucked body from the furs, and spears her in a single thrust. They both groan. She is open now, copious with slick and our combined cum. His body moves with fluid power, his cock splitting her wet pussy.

Nate is my blood. Watching him fuck her is like watching an extension of myself.

Dax fists her hair, lifting her face from the covers. She is flushed, lashes lowered, and mouth open—high on our pheromones and carnal attention.

She is an Omega in heat, and we are giving her what she needs.

"Fuck, your pussy is tight," Nate says. "Hot, tight, and slick." The sounds of his rutting are enough to harden my cock again.

Dax runs the tip of his thumb around her open lips before dipping it inside.

It slips out as Nate pulls her hips higher, canting her ass and finding the angle that makes her scream.

She is coming and what a glorious sight.

That sound is enough to have my dick spitting cum without a hint of stimulation. I grit my teeth, breathing heavily, determined that the only place my cum will go this night is inside her hot cunt.

But gods that scream, the contorted rapture on her face, and Nate's rough growls as he slams deep and holds.

They both groan, and he takes her chin in his hand, twisting her so he can capture her lips for a kiss, their tongues dueling while he fills her with cum.

His lips wrench from hers, finding the juncture of her throat and shoulder where I have already bitten.

He bites.

Her lips part and a silent scream, her slight body bucking underneath him

Dax growls, low and aggressive. He has waited, but his patience is exhausted.

Nate growls back, sinking his teeth deeper while tightening his grip on the little prey still locked on his knot. I put a hand on Dax's shoulder because he's wearing the look that says he is about to rip Nate off.

I don't worry about Nate. He's an Alpha half-wolf, and he can handle Dax—mostly. But I will not have them fighting over the helpless Omega or tearing out a locked knot.

Nate and Dax remain engaged in a glaring match, but I sense Dax has controlled his bestial side enough to wait.

Then Nate reaches under Belle. Dax and I both know he is strumming her clit. Her mouth opens, and a series of garbled syllables pour out.

I'm tense—we all are. Now I'm the one who wants to rip Nate off, but hell and damnation take me, she is begging him to make her come.

"Good girl, squeeze my knot, and I'll pet this needy little clit until you come."

I swallow; he has a fist wrapped around her long, fire-tipped auburn hair, arching her neck. Of the three of us, Nate is the one most practiced at charm—he also has a propensity for filthy talk that has gotten him under a girl's skirt as often as said charm.

I'm a little light-headed there is so much blood in my dick. Her breathing turns choppy. By the time he has finished his explicit rhetoric, she is screaming and spasming on the end of his dick.

Heavy breathing follows. All of us are breathing hard, and Dax hasn't even enjoyed her slick warmth yet.

Belle

Oh my gods, what has he done to me? The climax Nate has forced from my well-used body feels like it has taken my earthly soul.

I am limp and wrung out. My womb aches with of all of the cum pumped into me, but my greedy inner muscles pulse around the thick swelling as if to encourage more. It's softening a little, I think.

Nate's hands tighten on my hips, and he tugs against the tight sucking of my pussy. It stings, and I hiss out a complaint—it hasn't softened that much!

"Work it in and out," Dax states gruffly.

"Huh?" Nate grunts.

"The knot," Dax elaborates. "I don't want to tear her, and I'm hard as fucking stone after that fucking show you put on."

What? Work the knot in and out? Is he insane? "No!" My voice is a rasp after all my prior screaming.

"Good idea," Silas says like I'm not even here.

"Fuck, you're kidding me, right?" Nate says, testing his knot against the entrance. I clench harder—no, he can't do this! "Do you have any idea how fucking sensitive my knot is right now. I'm going to nut again in no time."

"Do the best you can," Dax growls. "And if you must come, make sure you keep your knot outside. The extra lubrication won't hurt."

"Please, no—"

I manage no more because Nate has already done it, and the thick swelling slips out.

"Fuck," Nate mutters as our combined juices splatter my legs and the furs. He jabs back in immediately. I hiss and curse him, trying to wriggle away—not that I have a hope—and less so when Dax takes my wrists within his huge hand and pins them to the bed.

"Good, keep working it," Dax says.

"Gods, please!" My wail accompanies Nate doing as instructed. The thick bulge of his knot is darkly erotic as it is forced in and out. I feel it stretching me, and my openness becomes a source of great distress. He's breaking me, and I'll never be the same.

Hot tears spring, even as my body rises toward another climax.

My tears do not move them. They are unwavering and united in this quest to open me. Dax is the only one who has kept his pants on, and I'm beginning to fear whatever he must be hiding.

Silas cups my chin, his thumb brushes my tears aside. His other hand squeezes my breast before he begins to pinch and tug my nipple in time with Nate's slow thrusts.

I am lost. I am a lone sapling being swept up in an avalanche.

Outside the small cottage, a storm is battering the walls. Inside, there is a different kind of storm. The three Alphas are the forces of nature, and all of them are acting upon me.

Nate

She has the sweetest pussy I've ever had. Tales abound of mating with an Omega, boasting of delights few can hope to obtain. The extreme sensitivity of my knot as I force it in and out of her slippery cunt has me hanging on by a thread. I almost wish it were Silas that Dax had made this demand of—it is a torment, but it's also a sublime form of ecstasy.

Her hot walls have opened under my administrations. There is little resistance to the swelling now, but I know she will still wail like a virgin when Dax claims her. She'll be well-used once he is done.

"Oh gods!"

Her squeal accompanies her pussy's fluttering, which soon morphs into the sweet, rhythmic contractions designed by the Goddess to coax a rutting male to release his seed.

I come. It is a powerful release, and I see stars. I feel like my entire body has just been expelled from the tip of my cock, the force is so great. My knot is still outside, and I fist it as best I can. The urge to slam it deep, is strong, but I retain sufficient wits to keep it outside.

"Fuck. Fuck. Fuck!" My balls ache. I have utterly drained them, but they still strain like they are trying to find more.

It is agonizing. It is glorious.

I'm so dazed that I don't notice Dax move until his thick fingers close around my neck to yank me off. My growl is aggressive, but that is as far as my complaint goes. My legs are so weak it's all I can do to make it back to the bed where I can collapse beside our Omega beauty.

Belle

My limit is far behind me, and yet I still want more. I am a vessel for their pleasure, and they haven't all taken their pleasure yet. This is the way of mating; I understand this. They are binding me to them, filling me with their seed. If the Goddess wills it, one of them will breed me before this night is done.

Distantly I'm aware that Dax has taken Nate's place. The youngest of the trio lays on his back beside me, chest heaving with gusty breaths.

The sight makes me smile.

Nate is young and beautiful, his nose regal, and his eyes, when he cracks them open to meet mine, are the color of summer skies. There is mischief to him, and I'm more convinced of this when he bestows on me a lazy smile.

"Brace yourself, Belle," he says and winks at me.

I face the soft-furred covers, but strong hands grip my hips, dragging me up and canting my back. A glance over my shoulder reveals the broad-chested Dax standing at the foot of the bed.

What is that thing?

I get no more than a peek at the ruddy-looking monstrosity jutting from between his legs when Silas takes my chin in his hand.

"Eyes forward, little one." His grip tightens when I try to take another look. I must have been imagining—I'm not myself, I am under the influence of heat.

Then the blunt tip is at my entrance, and I know what I saw is real.

"Not this way," Nate says. "She needs a better distraction, even during heat."

Dax growls, but his hands release my hip, and I'm turned onto my back.

Nate took me in the way of animals, and I'm disquieted by this suggestion. Of the three of them, Dax is the most distant, and I'm not ready for this intimacy . . . but I'm darkly interested, and no little amount fearful, of the pole he carries between his legs.

I do not have a choice.

I'm turned over, but before I can get a good look at the monster Dax is about to impale me with, a mouth lowers over mine. It's Silas.

There is a hunger in his kiss, and it steals all my thoughts. Lips are against my shoulder. Hands are roaming over my body everywhere. Soft kisses, gentle hands, and a rod, thicker than my arm, trying to force its way inside.

The pressure is relentless, and the kisses cannot hope to distract me. A hot mouth closes over my breast sucking gently upon the nipple sore from previous attention.

The club trying to enter me causes my back to arch off the bed.

I'm pinned and held perfectly still so that the thick head breeches the entrance with ease. Silas's tongue plunges into my mouth in an intimate imitation of sex as Dax's iron cock fills me inch by tormented inch.

My channel is so drenched that with each measured thrust, Dax surges deeper.

Despite my initial fear, it doesn't hurt. Not exactly pleasure, but not painful either. Instead, it builds an immense pressure.

I'm surrounded and penetrated. I am being opened and exposed. It is relentless and all-consuming. The hands roaming my body pinching and petting my dampened flesh are like flames.

They possess me, all three of them possess me in every way they can.

A wild groan escapes me, lost under the heady assault of Silas's kiss.

"Fuck!" Dax yells as he fills me, his crotch flush with mine, his muscular thighs holding mine open lewdly. He begins to rut me. It is different like this, but he's different and maybe that is part of it.

They are all unique in their loving of my body. Their interest is dark and carnal. They don't ask me for this, they take what they consider theirs.

Dax is taking me with slow, brutal thrusts. I'm helpless to do anything but accept him.

Goddess help me, his cock is monstrous. I am full beyond comfort, and yet it touches nerves in a way that unhinges all my self-control.

Fingers find the slippery, swollen nub of my clit, working over it mercilessly even as Dax growls over his prize. I gush around the invasion, and he slams in and out with wet slaps.

"Gods, that is a vision of depravity," Nate says, voice roughened with lust. "Look how she takes him. He's using her pussy so well."

Lips pop off mine. Silas's head twists so he can see down my body. Nate cups the back of my neck, lifting my head, and I blink in lust drunk confusion as I try to take in all the moving parts.

Silas lays stretched out to my right, his fingers toying lazily with my nipple, plucking and pulling it. Nate lays stretched out to my left, my nipple wet and stiff where he has been sucking on it. It is Nate's fingers that pinch and slide over my sensitive clit.

Between my spread legs, Dax kneels. His vast bulk of rippling muscle working as he pumps. Goddess, that cock—I tip over into a climax. My lashes flutter closed, behind them is emblazoned the vision of him pounding into me.

It is obscene, *debauched*.

A scream leaves my lips as my inner muscles fight to contract around his immense girth. He slams deep with a savage growl, and the terrible pressure rises higher still.

There is still the knot. How can I possibly take his knot?

I don't have a choice. He isn't giving me a choice, none of them are. Held immobile, I can only lay open and receive.

My contractions have barely stopped when the knot drives me into another round. A sting burns my neck—the claiming mark—Dax is also claiming me. This time it's sharper, higher. The pleasure is everywhere, a thread between my clit, nipples and the claiming mark, and a fire bathing over my skin.

I lose consciousness.

When I awake, I'm draped over a warm body, another lays at my side. I ache everywhere, and yet I'm sated and safe.

All three of them have mated me, and awareness blooms inside. Too tired to explore it, I take comfort from it as I drift into sleep.

CHAPTER THIRTEEN

Dax

"Good boy!" Nate calls as Shep hobbles after the stick Nate throws.

I don't know who has taken to who more, Nate or the damn mutt.

The dog is walking now—he tries to run, but he's not there yet.

"I thought it would be easier once we'd fucked her," I say. I am staring at the mutt, but I'm thinking about Belle. Her heat broke this morning. For the last six days, one of us has been buried balls-deep in her hot cunt at all times. Today is the first time we have left the bedding nook to do more than the necessary.

"I think it's worse," Silas agrees. "My dick is still hard. The only reason I left the bed is the fear I would rut her again when she woke up. That I was prepared to wait for her to wake told me I was coming out of my rut."

I nod. "My legs are weak," I say. "I wasn't this wrecked after the weeklong battle at Sorem Bridge."

But Silas isn't listening, for the cottage door has been flung open.

"Fuck," he mutters as Belle steps out. She wears her dress, but it is barely buttoned and her tits threaten to spill out. Silas burned every pair of her pants and underthings the morning after the attack while mumbling about 'ease of access'.

There are times when I appreciate why he is first Alpha.

"How did she survive this long on her own?" he mutters before roaring, "Belle!"

She freezes. I wince since I'm closest to the source of his roar. Even the mutt flattens himself to the ground and pins his ears to his head.

"Put your fucking shoes on!"

She glares at him. We are a reasonable distance apart, but I can clearly see the mulish set to her jaw, and it will not serve her well.

"Nate! Discipline Belle."

Fists planted on her hips, she stares Silas down.

"What the fuck?" Nate mutters, running a hand through his messy hair.

Belle stomps back into the home, returning shortly later wearing shoes—unfastened.

"I don't want to fucking discipline her," Nate complains bitterly as he approaches. He's glaring at me like it's my fault Silas has made this determination. The mutt, sensing the burgeoning hostility, slinks off to his bedding area in the barn.

Nate and Silas engage in a heated argument about Belle's impending discipline. I'm amazed Silas doesn't bloody his nose and be done with it.

I'm contemplating following the mutt into the barn when Nate ceases his whining tirade abruptly.

"Wait?" Nate says, glancing over his shoulder to where Belle disappeared to go about her business. "She's been gone for a long time."

Silas growls. He doesn't need to tell me.

I go.

I expect her to have run. I don't know why I assume this, but I do.

Instead, I find her waiting behind the house, arms folded across her chest, tapping her toe impatiently.

"I want you to know that this time I thought about it," she says.

I don't mean to smile at her naughtiness, but I can't help myself. I still toss her over my shoulder and carry her back to the house.

Nate has a bloody nose when I pass him at the bottom of the steps and is pinching the bridge in an attempt to stem the flow.

"Where the fuck did you learn that?" I swat Belle's ass when she issues a particularly filthy curse. "That is no way to talk about Nate's mother."

Dropping her to the floor before the hearth, I glare down at her. She glares back but seeing Nate unbuckling his belt, the color drains from her face. "What are you doing?" she demands in a high, anxious voice, although I'm confident she knows what Nate is doing.

She tries to bolt.

Nate scoops her up. "This is for your own good," he says, his tone brooking no argument. I admit, he has a way about him when it comes to her discipline—he has really come into his own.

"Do not make her come," Silas says.

Nate stops—Belle is bent over the table, squeals muffled by the dress that Nate has tossed over her. "Can I fuck her?"

"No," Silas says thickly. "And don't take all day about it, I need you to scout."

Her ass is jiggling about as she struggles, and I'm deaf to the next part of the conversation.

Then I zone back in . . .

" . . . and why the fuck does Dax get to comfort her after? He hasn't disciplined her once!"

Silas doesn't answer, and I sense he will do more than bloody the whelp's nose if he doesn't obey the order.

With a huff of defeat, Nate picks up his belt and sets about welting her ass. "You know better than to the leave the house with no shoes on," he says between blows. "And giving Silas attitude is a sure road to suffering—as I would know." His tirade is somewhat muted by the blocked state of his bloody nose.

But I'm too busy worrying about the fact that I must comfort her. I'll end up rutting her, and then *I* will lose dick privileges for a week.

By the time he's done, she is sobbing in earnest. Nate glares at Silas as he helps her pull her dress down and all but thrusts her at me.

"I want Nate!" she says, and it's like a knife stabbing into my chest.

"Nate needs to scout," Silas states. "We are leaving tomorrow, and we need to prepare."

She falls to sobbing at this news.

Tension grips the room. In his wolf form, Nate could best Silas, but he's not in his wolf form, and he has never once shifted during an altercation.

Although his wolf is deadly, it's controlled by animal instincts, and he cannot lead us in that form.

His human form is not a leader, either.

We all know we must soon leave. If we stay here, we won't survive, news we all know will hurt Belle. Yet it's Silas who is the one to deliver this without hesitation. By giving the order to move on, he takes Belle's displeasure upon himself.

As he does when he orders Nate to see to her discipline.

Although Nate delivers the punishment, the young Omega within our care understands that he's only doing what he is told.

I had my doubts that Nate would bond with Belle, but now I

think their bond might be the strongest.

Despite the many occasions when the whelp vexes me and I want to cuff him for his whining, he is my brother, and it would sadden me if he wasn't part of our collective bond. Perhaps Silas insisted upon Nate taking this disciplinary role because he knew it would cement the bond.

Or perhaps this is merely a consequence of other reasoning.

It isn't easy to be first Alpha, and harder still for Silas since he was not firstborn and so was forced to defer to Bram.

There have been times when I envy Silas his role, but many more when I do not.

"I am not stupid," Belle says. "I understand we need to leave. But you don't need to be a brute about how you tell me!"

A tic thumps in Silas's jaw—he is pissed.

Nate stomps out. I don't blame him, there is a strong possibility that Silas might order him to add welts to her already flaming ass.

Silas narrows his eyes, and I pull her closer against me in a protective move. Nate might be gone, but Silas could still call him back.

He could also order me to do it.

My hands are big and capable of terrible things, but they are gentle as I try to soothe her wild tears and trembling. Pulling her face into my chest, I offer up my purr. Her bottom is well striped from Nate's belt, and I have no desire to add more.

"She is lingering with heat," I say. "She doesn't mean to challenge you."

"He is a beast and a brute, and I do!"

Goddess help us, she will test us all with her defiance.

This outburst brings a wry smile to Silas, and the tension drops. So it surprises me when he steps into her, fists her hair to arch her neck back so he can look her in the eye.

The move pins her between our larger bodies. Her breathy gasp is pure arousal.

"Do not test me, Omega," he growls. "Not while I'm still half in rut, or you will find yourself taken in ways you are not yet ready to endure."

Her tears have dried up, and when her chest heaves, I can feel her hardened nipples where her tits are mashed up against me.

Her submission to his aggression and dominance is a heady thing, and when he tightens his fist on her hair, her moan sends blood pooling in my dick.

Lifting his eyes from the arresting sight, Silas pins me with a glare. "Do not fuck her," he says before stalking out the door.

The door slams shut with a crash.

"I don't want to leave," she says quietly.

"I know, Belle," I say. Lifting her, I take her to the bedding nook. There is a small, weak fight on her part before she allows me to comfort her. "There isn't enough food for one person, even supposing we could eat the pigs," I say reasonably. A little huff escapes her lips at the mention of pigs—it's a sore point. "Game is scarce, and it will soon be nonexistent. Had we not chanced upon you, you would have needed to leave or you would have perished here alone."

It puts me in a dark mood to think of her struggling.

"You are Imperium Guards," she says. "Where will we go?"

"We are bonded mates to an Omega now," I reply. "We will go to our family home."

I don't tell her about the trouble that awaits us there. Bram is firstborn, and an Alpha much enamored with himself and his lot. I can't see him taking to the news of our arrival well, but that is a matter for another time.

"Will you tell me about it?" she asks.

It has been several years since I was home, but the memories are emblazoned on my mind. I'm an Imperium guard. I expected to die in my duty, as many of my guard-brothers have. If I survived to old age by some miracle, I would likely take on a training role in the barracks until my days were done.

I never expected to return home in a manner of permanency. Alphas are by nature aggressive, and firstborn or first Alphas doubly so.

When an Omega is claimed, all unmated brothers within the family have a right to be part of that claim. Where they sit on the hierarchy decides their privileges. Bram will not welcome the challenge we bring to his status quo. He is the lord of our family home, first born, and he will want autonomy over the Omega.

I'm confident in Silas, and I grin to myself as I contemplate Bram's future life adjustments.

It's not a future I hoped or wished for. It's a thousand times better. There will be bumps along the way, not least our journey home and the ensuing conflict between Silas and Bram.

But the little Omega is troubled enough, so I tell her all the good things about our future home, and leave the other parts aside.

CHAPTER FOURTEEN

Nate

The pig weighs a fucking ton.

"Don't hurt her!"

My eyes roll heavenward, and I curse as I wrestle a screaming pig onto the cart. Dax is waiting beside the cart, watching my antics with a grim expression somewhere between sadistic joy and torture. This is payback for when Silas made him recapture the one I tried to butcher.

I've spent the whole of yesterday in preparation for the journey. We're packed, the horses are ready—Belle is as ready as she will ever be—all that's left is the fucking pigs.

"He understands," Silas says in his reasonable tone. It's fine for him to be reasonable, he isn't the one wrestling with the fucking pig! I never liked pig, my wolf now fucking hates them—and I'm confident I will never eat pork again.

"Please don't . . . Oh, he's going to hurt them!"

For fat lumps they possess a cantankerous level of demonic

power when they don't want to do something. Heaving the last pig inside, I turn and stalk toward Belle while reaching for my belt.

Her eyes, wide with fear, drop to watch me unbuckle and draw the loop of leather out as I close in. Swallowing, she backs up into Silas with a squeak.

"Do not stop me," I growl, but Silas only looks on, amused, as I fist her arm and haul her toward the barn.

"What are you doing?" she wails, although I'm confident she knows exactly what I'm about to do.

"Do not tell a man how to put a fucking pig into a cart!"

I toss her over the nearest bale of hay and shove her dress up to expose her jiggling ass. She's squirming and fighting, but I pin her securely and set about welting her ass. She squeals and rails at me, but I'm sorely irritated. I mete out a dozen sharp licks of the leather before freeing the hot, heavy, weight of my cock and plunging it into her dripping cunt.

With my fist in her hair to hold her still, I rut her while telling her how little I like her instructing me on how to do my jobs. I'll take that from Silas, he is first Alpha after all, but I will not take instructions from a woman.

I'm using her roughly, but an Omega was meant to take an Alpha's aggression, and her pussy gushes around me. She fights and wails her protests, but the wet, slapping sounds of our fierce coupling tell a different story.

The speed with which I knot her might be a source of embarrassment under different circumstances. As my nuts rise, my brain completely shuts down, and I empty myself inside her with a growl. I exist in a state of rapture that cares nothing of naughty Omegas or bad-tempered pigs.

"No!" she says.

I chuckle. I don't mean to let my amusement show, but jetting my cum into her hot sheath drains my temper.

"No!" she repeats.

And my mood has been passed directly onto Belle. She's not unhappy about the knot, so much, more that she hasn't gotten to come.

"If you knew how much I hate those pigs, you would take your punishment and be quiet about it."

She's not quiet about it. And her cursing could make a sailor blush.

"Get it out!"

Her wriggling earns her a smack on her reddened ass. "If you want to come, ask nicely and I'll consider it."

She struggles harder, and I fear she may actually rip the knot out. Sighing loudly, I pin her tightly against the bale of hay lest she hurt herself. "I do not want to reward your naughtiness, but you'll be in a foul mood all day if I don't sort this out."

"What? No!" Her wail of outrage accompanies me getting my fingers on her clit. It's swollen and slippery, and her continued struggles cause her to squeeze and gush around my cock and knot.

I see stars long before her expressions of outrage turn to wild moans of pleasure as her pussy spasms in climax. By the time she's done, I'm close to passing out from the overstimulation of my already sensitized cock.

We both breathe gusty breaths in the aftermath, and I grin because she is now adorably limp and sated. I like that I made her so.

"If you two have finished," Silas says from the barn doorway. "We need to get moving."

The knot has softened, but the act of withdrawing from her hot cunt still makes me shudder. She wails as my cum spills out and snatches down her dress. Face as red as her flaming hair, she stomps off out of the barn.

I'm still grinning even after Silas cuffs the back of my head.

Belle

I want to clean myself up, but Silas doesn't allow it. Fisting my arm, he directs me over to the cart where I'm dumped beside Dax, who waits, reins in his hands. Shep is in the footwell, tail thumping excitedly at my arrival.

"I'm sticky!" I complain. I'm fully exasperated by Nate's rough treatment, and my bottom is also very sore.

"I don't care," Silas says. "You're still lingering with heat—expect to be fucked often."

My wide-eyed gasp of outrage does nothing to soften his expression; if anything, his jaw tightens. I'm convinced he's about to snatch me from the cart and begin fucking me then and there, when Dax flicks the reins and Percy lumbers forward.

His jaw is also tight . . . and my eyes lower before I can counsel myself to the telling bulge in his pants.

I swallow.

"Do not stare at it unless you need a closer inspection," Dax says.

As my lashes flash up, I see a smirk on his lips.

I didn't know the man possessed a sense of humor! He picked a poor time to show it.

With a huff, I face forward. But I only manage my facade for a short time before I sneak a peek over my shoulder. A pang of intense emotions well up inside. They keep telling me it's the lingering effects of my heat, but I know that it is more.

I don't want to leave; it's my home . . . it is the last place I saw my father.

Perhaps sensing the rising tide of renewed grief, Shep shuffles in the footwell to lay his head upon my lap. I pet his silky ears and thank the Goddess that he is still with me. It still upsets me to see the chunk missing—his battle scar, as Nate calls it.

I remember him as a pup when my father brought him home after a local farmer's bitch had a litter. He was small, wriggly, and bandy on his legs, and I loved him instantly.

He is older now, and although he's not as old as Percy, my time with him is also precious. "My brave boy," I say while ruffling the fur at the nape of his neck. Unlike his ears, which are soft and silky, the fur here is coarse and wiry.

I miss my father.

I think he would have approved of my three Alphas. They are fierce and protective, and they're not unkind . . . although I might wish they were a little less ready to use the belt.

And the other things . . . I fidget in my seat, thinking about what Nate has just done. I don't understand why he is the one who always disciplines me.

I don't know why I get so hot and needy when he does.

I sneak another glance back. Dax's horse is tethered to the back of the cart. Nate and Silas are mounted and nudge their horses to follow behind.

This is happening. We are leaving.

It is a three day trip to the nearest village, the town, another week.

They are the furthest places I have been since we arrived so many years ago. There are vague memories of another home far away, of a mother with golden hair, and a kitchen where they baked crusty bread.

My mother died long ago, birthing my baby brother.

He died too.

I don't remember much about it now, but my father said the shock triggered my dynamic to reveal, and we left within a matter of days.

The cottage was abandoned when we arrived, and so much of my father's sweat went into making it a home. My heart weeps to see the place empty once again.

"Look ahead, Belle," Dax says, and I drag my tear-filled gaze away.

Ahead, the path is nearly overgrown, but it will connect to a broader track in a few miles. Half-a-day further, we will meet the rutted road that leads to the village.

My glance at Dax shows a stolid expression—he's not a man who shows emotions readily, and yet I believe, despite his quietness, he feels much.

He's talking about more than the narrow, bramble-edged path before us, he is talking about the future I have with my three mates. I have dedicated a great deal of the time while I was packing my meager essentials to imagining their home after Dax described it to me.

But there are also aspects of that magical home that have left me concerned. When I asked him who lived there now, his answer was *evasive*.

I pet Shep's silky ear—the one that was not cut by the bandit's sword—and contemplate what is next.

CHAPTER FIFTEEN

Nate

It takes us three days to reach the village. The pathways between Belle's former home and the nearest pocket of civilization are poor quality and rutted, and the cart, full of overfed pigs, bogs down often.

I'm a soldier of the Imperium, getting in the dirt to free trapped carts full of demonic pigs is not a task I ordinarily care for.

The pigs hate me.

We can't afford to let them down or we might never get them back in. So I'm forced to use the brute strength of half-shift whenever a wheel gets stuck. Half-shift is challenging to maintain and uses enormous amounts of energy. It instills a cantankerous level of mutiny in the pigs, and they squeal and roll their eyes the entire time, while stamping around in the small space on their short, fat legs.

I fucking hate the pigs, but after the third time of straining to free the cart, I'm so hungry I'm ready to rip the guts out of the nearest sow and feast on its entrails.

"Nate!" Silas's barked command snaps my head around, and I shift back to human.

"Go and hunt," he says.

I belatedly notice that the pigs are climbing over one another in a frenzied attempt to escape the cart's confines. Belle is white as death and clinging to Dax. Silas, who was wedging a small plank under the muddy ground beside me, is glaring, nostrils flared and radiating every bit of his first Alpha power.

The nearest pig might have been clawed a bit—there is a distinct mark in its plump pink flesh.

I shift, my clothes crumple to the ground, and I bound off into the nearby forest searching for prey.

It takes me a while, but I snag a hare who was foolish enough to forage in the last of the autumn sun. It's little more than a snack, but I'm hungry and take what I can. It takes the edge of, and I lope back to the pathway to find the cart lumbering into the small village as dusk closes in.

I shift before I reach the cart, lest I send the pigs into another frenzy. Jogging over, I snag my clothes, which have been dumped into the cart footwell. Belle gives me a wary look before staring pointedly ahead. Even the mutt isn't impressed.

I hop alongside the cart, dressing, and fighting a sense of resentment. There's only a bit of blood in the back . . . and the pig is still alive.

I get my boots on as the cart lumbers to a stop beside a rickety farmhouse. The village isn't really a village, more a small collection of farms that are in reasonable proximity to each other. There is sufficient labor for the cluster of homes to have sprung up over the years to support them.

The village boasts two taverns and a church, all of which are in a sorry state. Few people pass through such remote locations, and our arrival causes interest from the grubby children playing in the lane.

"Maybe we should take them with us," Belle says while staring at the pigs like this is a good option.

This isn't a good option. It's taken us several long and arduous days to reach this backwater village. The weather is close to turning for winter, and the prospect of carting nine overfed pigs plus feed all the way to our home on the other side of the Empire is a test beyond measure.

She turns expectantly to Silas, who has drawn his horse to a stop beside the cart. I've never envied Silas his mantle of first Alpha and particularly not today.

He grunts and heaves a sigh. They have had this conversation several times since he announced we were leaving. She's either brave, foolhardy, or desperate since the discussion usually results in him ordering me to welt her ass.

I sigh and reach for my belt.

Silas surprises me by shaking his head. "Later," he says.

Her head whips around before her eyes rest on my buckle where my hand is paused. "I was only discussing it!"

"You were not discussing it," Silas says gruffly. "We were discussing it the first time, the subsequent seventeen times were arguing—which is why you got the belt."

Her face turns red with outrage, even though she knows she was arguing.

We're distracted from this altercation when a heavily pregnant woman waddles over and takes the nearest lad by the ear. "Go an' get your father," she says—the lad, who'd had another lad in a headlock, whoops and sprints off.

The headlock victim staggers to his feet and, issuing a battle cry, charges after him.

Belle jumps down and goes over to greet the woman. They must know each other because they hug before they begin talking.

Silas dismounts, and Dax climbs down, lifting the mutt to the ground. He can't jump, but he's been keeping up with the horses well enough whenever we let him stretch his legs. The horse will be bartered, along with the pigs and the cart. There is also a small bit of feed. Not even Silas was brave enough to suggest leaving Shep behind, so we'll have to manage as best we can.

A stout farmer emerges from behind the building, bald of head and thick of beard.

Silas begins negotiating.

He's having a hard time of it, negotiating with country farmers is not Silas's forte. The farmer eyeballs the pigs, expression turning from gleeful to sour as the deal is laid out.

"Do not kill the fucking pigs or I swear I will come back and gut you," Silas growls.

The farmer's face blanches.

A bag of coins is passed over . . . but from Silas to the farmer, who is clearly not happy about housing nine, fat pigs and neither money nor threat is helping.

The farmer scratches his jaw. "You want me to keep the pigs? For how long?" He weighs up the threat Silas is laying out. Wondering if the Imperium Guard and Alpha looming over him really will come back and disembowel him should the pigs not be kept in perfect health. "What am I supposed to do with them?" He finally says.

"Feed them," Silas mutters, shoving another bag of coin into his hand.

I believe the threat and coin are good for a year . . . it's more than the pigs deserve.

"What has happened to them?" The farmer nudges his head at the blood-smeared cart. "Has a wolf been at them? I take no account for them coming to me damaged."

"Shifter," Silas nudges his head at me.

I grin.

The farmer drops his coin bag on the floor, crouching and fumbling for it without taking his eyes from me.

Dax huffs out a breath as he cuffs the back of my head.

"What?" I glare at him.

"Stop fucking with the farming folk," he grunts and stomps off to untether his horse from the back. Shep, who has sat at my feet, looks up at me expectantly, his tail drumming against the floor.

Silas is still talking to the farmer. We need a horse for Belle, but we're not going to get one here from the look of things. That's okay. She's small and the extra weight won't trouble our mounts much . . . and I can always run.

The farmer finally nods and calls one of his men over to begin unloading the pigs. He's taken the money now, so he doesn't have much choice.

Also, Silas has a way about him that can make the toughest Beta wilt.

"You've been fleeced," Dax says when Silas joins us.

"I know," Silas replies. "But it's an unreasonable request, and I don't have the heart for it. I'm glad to be rid of them."

I nod—we're in agreement on that point. If I never see a pig again for the rest of my life I'll be happy.

My focus shifts to the little Omega we have claimed as ours. My stomach rumbles. I'm still hungry after the many half-shifts, but I'm distracted by a different kind of hunger, one that involves lifting Belle's skirts and getting my dick into her tight sheath.

"Let's get something to eat," Silas states gruffly. He is also staring at Belle.

We're all staring at Belle like we are ravenous and she's the only sustenance we need.

She throws a casual glance over her shoulder but, seeing us staring, her mouth pops open on a gasp that brings a tightness to my balls.

A bawdy group of farmhands round the building, heading for the tavern, and it breaks the spell. We passed through here while pursuing Oswold before we stumbled on the little cottage where Belle lived alone. The tavern serves plain but tasty food, and the beer is strong, unlike the cities where they tend to water it down.

"When are you going to tell her about Bram?" I ask, not taking my eyes from Belle.

There is a stretched silence. Bram can't be ignored forever—he is the resident lord of our family home. If he yields to Silas, he will have his share of our Omega . . . but if he doesn't, it could result in conflict.

It's bold of me to question Silas, and I'm half-expecting a cuff or bloody nose.

He huffs. "When I'm ready—let's eat." But like all of us, I believe he's already thinking about what happens afterward.

Belle

It has been a year since I have seen Merel, and she has had another child during this time! And from the size of her swollen belly, there's another one due any day. There are no Alphas in the village, only Betas, and although an Omega scent is appealing, it doesn't drive a Beta mad with lust.

I have visited with my father many times, and it is good to see familiar faces, even if it is for the last time.

The night is drawing in, and the tavern is lit with a cheery glow. I've eaten here by day when I visited with my father. It was quieter then, but there is an enticing rowdiness to it tonight. While I'm content on my own, I have missed these simple interactions.

I glance over my shoulder, wondering if we'll stay the night.

My breath catches in my throat as I find my three Alphas staring at me like I'm dinner, and they're about to feast. Seeing them stand together, I'm struck by both the similarities and differences between them. They are each strong, powerful, worthy mates.

Goddess, just looking at them leaves me breathless and needy. When we camped on the side of the path, they each took me, thrusting my skirts up and rutting me from behind on my hands and knees with only my cloak as a cushion.

I don't care how they take me, only that they do. I'm greedy for their attention, for them to put their hands on me and their cocks in me and make me feel good. Silas says that I need to be rutted often so that my scent stays muted, and I'm safe.

There is more to the compulsion than that. I see them eyeing me and sense the tension building the longer the day goes on.

I feel the echo of them inside me, even when they're not.

Merel chuckles. "They are fearsome mates," she says, drawing my attention back to her. "But it heartens me to see you'll be well cared for now that your father is gone." Her hand rubs over her belly. "I'm due any day, and I need a moment off my feet! Take care, lovey." She kisses my cheek and squeezes me in a tight hug before collaring her little rascals and ordering them see to our horses and Shep.

An inelegant yip escapes my parted lips when I glance back and find Silas stalking toward me. I'm reminded all over again of his towering presence as he bears down upon me.

They're all bearing down upon me, and it's overwhelming.

I'm ready to turn and run when Silas fists my arm. He drags my body flush with his, spears his big hand into my hair, and kisses me breathless. His roughened beard, the softness of his lips, and the tongue plundering my mouth, send my heart racing and a heat sweeping over my skin.

His scent and presence fill my world. I cling, wanting nothing more than him to thrust me to the rough ground and fuck me then and there.

He rips his mouth from mine. I suck in much-needed air, blinking and swaying, aware of Nate and Dax watching.

"Food," he mutters. Taking my small hand in his, he leads me toward the tavern.

Inside, it's boisterous and loud. I shrink back, only to collide with Dax. His big hand settles on my shoulder.

"There's a table," Silas says, pointing to the far side of the room. We squeeze through the merry farming folks to the round booth. I'm squished between Silas and Dax, and I feel very safe as I watch the revelry.

Nate stops to chat with a man at the bar—they appear to know each other.

A buxom serving woman slams tankards of beer on the table before us.

"Oh." My eyes grow round. I've never tasted beer before, but I'm curious and immediately pick it up, nose wrinkling at the sickly aroma of overripe fruit.

"I don't think this is such a good idea," Dax says, gesturing at me as he sips his beer.

I take a big gulp lest he decides to take it away.

Goddess save me, it's awful, bitter, and disturbingly gloopy.

It hits my stomach like a rock. I swallow it as quickly as I can despite an instinctive urge to spit it out. Silas chuckles, the beast thinks this is funny!

"Is there something wrong with it?" I ask seriously.

He laughs harder.

I'm distracted from his ridicule by the activity within the tavern. There is a great deal of raucous laughter and shouting. People are very friendly . . . especially with the young servers.

"Oh," I say as I notice what one young man is doing to a serving maid.

"This wasn't a good idea," Dax grumbles.

"Leann! Bring me another beer!" a man shouts, slapping the serving maid on her ample ass. She smacks his hand away, but she's laughing and doesn't appear to be offended.

Nate finishes with his conversation and turns toward the table when a nearby serving maid squeals and throws herself at him.

I blink as I take in the pair of them. She has fully launched herself into his arms, and his hands, as he stumbles backward, have landed on her ass.

I didn't think I had an aggressive bone in my body, but as I watch her clinging to Nate and pressing kisses to his face, I desperately want to claw her eyes out with my short blunt nails.

That Nate peels her off with a thunderous expression is of small consequence against my rage. Silas curses, and Dax snags me around the waist when I make to crawl over the table to bloody this woman who touches what is mine.

Dax shakes me, but I'm like a feral kitten.

Nate sits, eyeing me warily.

"Well done, whelp," Dax says. He has to release an arm from around me so he can thump Nate.

Seizing the opportunity, I wrench free. I have straddled Nate's lap and sunk my small teeth into his throat before anyone can stop me.

"Ah fuck," Nate says, his fingers cupping the back of my neck. He doesn't try to pull me off; if anything, he encourages me to bite harder. "I'm sorry, Belle."

He swears again as I get my hand on his buckle. My dress is rucked up, and I have nothing else in the way of me and his hardening length. I need only undo this buckle to be filled how I need and crave.

The air leaves my lungs as I find myself on my back against the table. Nate's lips are against my throat as his fingers take over the task of freeing his hot cock.

"She's not a tavern wench!" Silas growls.

I'm hoisted up into Nate's arms, and he carries me out of the door. It's quieter outside, but not by much. More farmworkers are arriving, and it's close to full darkness. Lips covering mine, Nate weaves a zig-zag path around the side of the building. Here, he slams me against the wall, hand shaking as he fumbles between us so he can finally free himself.

He spears me in a single thrust.

Our ragged breaths mingle—I'd been mindless for the need to feel him inside me, but now everything is clear. "Yes, yes, yes!" This is what I need, what I needed hours ago. I pepper urgent kisses to his throat and face as he ruts me against the wall, pausing to drag my legs higher around his waist, opening me so he can fill me deeper.

"Fuck!" His thrusts are erratic against my franticness until he tightens his hold and begins to thrust into me hard and fast.

Ripping his shirt open, I gouge a path down his chest with my blunt nails.

"Yes!" He groans as he hammers me into the wall. "Mark me up. I swear I won't shift for the rest of my fucking life."

He doesn't want to lose the mark when he next shifts, and I scratch and bite harder like that might make it stick, delighting when my aggression only drives him to be rougher with me.

Then I feel it, the swelling at the base. Palming my throat, he takes my lips in a drugging kiss, thrusting his tongue in time with the slower tempo as he works the growing knot in and out.

I'm sliding deeper with every moment, my fingers fisting in his hair because I need an anchor in this storm. The stuttering of my breath precedes the fluttering inside my core. A sweet throb rises with every passage of the knot over sensitized nerves, while every slap of his body against mine strokes the little nub between my legs

I am both lost and found. I am the subject of a magical force the Goddess herself has bestowed upon me that I might be shown love through this earthly body I possess.

My cries of joyous rapture are caught within the kiss. The knot locks, and my well-used pussy convulses around Nate's thick rod.

We have barely met, and yet I know I love him. The memory of that woman daring to touch him only makes me grip harder.

Lifting his lips from mine, he stares down at me, eyes bright in the weak light.

"You are mine," I say. "I'm claiming you. When I was in heat, you might presume to be the one making a claim. But it is done now, and I've bitten you. It won't matter if you shift, the meaning of it is still there."

His lips tug up, and he chuckles, a low, husky sound that I would like more if he were not amused at my expense.

His smile fades when he notes my displeasure. "Sweet Belle," he says sincerely. "I accept your claim. I will always cherish you. I would give my life to protect you gladly because, without you, I would have none."

Inside, his softening length kicks with interest, and he groans. "See what you do to me. I swear your pussy was designed by the Goddess herself to fit perfectly around my cock."

We are interrupted by a growl.

Nate doesn't look over his shoulder, his focus is still on me. But he smirks as he withdraws, and the cum he just filled me with splatters out.

I don't need to look either to recognize that growl. It's Silas, and he hasn't yet had his turn tonight. But as I am lowered to the ground, it isn't Silas, but Dax who scoops me up and tosses me over his shoulder.

My squeal earns me a swat to my bottom, and as I peer up, I see

Silas following.

It seems I won't get to experience more of the tavern, for I'm carried off to the nearest barn where my other Alphas take their turn.

CHAPTER SIXTEEN

Silas

We rise early and leave the village minus the pigs, farm horse, and cart. The mutt is keeping up well enough, and we are finally taking our Omega prize to our home where she belongs.

All these things should put me in a good mood.

I'm not in a good mood. I am in a foul mood. I have ordered Nate to discipline her numerous times since we left the village and haven't allowed him to fuck her once.

Belle sits in front of me on the horse. Nate is scouting ahead in wolf form—she could have his horse, but I find I like her close. She's fidgeting after this morning's session with the strap. Mostly, it's been Nate's hand, but today as we close in on the town after a week of travel, I ordered him to use the strap.

I swear there was no blood left in my brain by the time he'd raised welts. After, I took her hard and fast and didn't let her come.

No one is happy with me—I'm not happy with myself, but it's all

I can do not to throw her to the ground and fuck her all over again.

"I want to walk for a while," she says and is halfway out of the saddle before I can toss her back before me.

"Do you need to feel the strap again?"

My question is met by silence, but she is openly seething. She doesn't want to be next to me. She wants Nate and has told me as much several times.

"It isn't the whelp's fault," Dax says reasonably. He's riding beside me since the forest path here is wide enough for us both.

"What isn't Nate's fault?" Belle demands.

Nate is scouting ahead. I'm glad he's out of earshot since he doesn't need further cause to gloat. I scowl at Dax, not appreciating his pearls of wisdom in this matter. The truth is, I'm jealous of the whelp.

No, jealous isn't a strong enough word for the rage that engulfs me.

I'm first Alpha, but I am second born. I have never asked for more than what I've been given, and yet hearing her earnest claiming words spoken to Nate was like being gutted with a blunt knife.

I am first, and those words should have been mine.

"You're holding me too tight!"

She has a healthy disregard for danger. It doesn't matter that I'm a male many times bigger and stronger; Belle is unperturbed and defiant.

"He isn't here," she says smugly. "You'll need to punish me yourself . . . or make Dax do it if you are not Alpha enough."

I growl. Now she's baiting me. It makes matters worse when Dax poorly disguises his laughter with a cough.

I pull the horse to a stop. Her squeal instills a sadistic level of joy as I haul her to the ground. The mutt is used to these antics and slinks off in disgust. Pinning her to the ground, I toss her skirts up and begin spanking her ass. It's not until I have landed a good number of firm swats, and both cheeks are a bright, cherry red, that I notice she's moaning and jiggling her ass to meet every strike.

Her bottom must be sore from this morning's discipline with the belt. By rights, she should be begging for mercy, not enticing me to give her more. I have engaged in a battle of wills with this little slip of a girl, and I'm in grave danger of losing.

I've been hard all day, and the need to fill her in every way I can with my cum is a fierce imperative. She moans in anticipation when I free my belt and take my cock in hand, but it is not her hot cunt that will be getting it today. Fisting her hair, I pull her mouth toward my aching shaft. "Open up."

Although I have never taken her like this before, she shows not a hint of hesitation. The air is cool even at midday at this time of year, and the sensation of her warm mouth closing over the tip and the swirl of her tongue as she collects the pre-cum is enough to render me temporarily blind.

Every part of her is small, including her mouth, but I don't let that stop me from forcing my length deeper.

She stares at me the whole time, eyes half-lidded with pleasure as I roughly take her mouth.

Her sharp tongue is being put to better use as she licks around my thrusting rod like it's a heaven-sent treat.

Truth be told, I don't mind her sass. I don't mind anything about her. I fall more deeply under her Goddess-blessed spell every day. I have no desire for a simpering female who is afraid to speak her mind.

Belle isn't afraid of anything or anyone. She's brave and has the heart of a warrior beating inside the small cage of her ribs. I loved her when I first saw her wet and bedraggled on the hearth, boldly meeting my eyes. I loved her impossibly more when she took the blunt knife from the table and cut through the bindings holding Nate while vicious outlaws surrounded her.

And I loved her as wholly as a mate can love when she gave her body to me for the first time.

Lust and love provide a potent aphrodisiac as I watch the debauched image of my large cock shuttling in and out of her hot mouth.

But I need her to claim me.

"Lift your skirts," I say roughly. "I want Dax to enjoy the sight of your well-disciplined ass while I'm filling your naughty mouth."

Still meeting my eyes, she reaches back to lift her skirts.

I'm focusing on the kneeling Omega who is sucking me off, but I'm also aware of Dax standing behind her and of the tense lines of his body.

"Are you wet, Belle? Do you need Dax to use your cunt while I use your pretty mouth?"

She hums around me, her bottom canting and jiggling to entice Dax. He doesn't need further encouragement. The mere sight of her exposed ass and wet folds has him falling to his knees behind her. He grips her hip in one hand to still her as he frees his cock with the other.

He's hung like a bull, and seeing this thick, ruddy rod being forced into her is nearly enough for me to come. I grit my teeth, determined to enjoy this first time we take her together.

She gasps and groans around my cock, struggling to keep her eyes on me as Dax begins to use her young body for his pleasure.

I cannot hope to hold back. Her scalp must be aching where I fist her hair to force her on and off my iron length. She's like a rag-doll being pushed and pulled on and off as we take our pleasure.

A primal roar of satisfaction and possession erupts from my chest as I spill my cum down her throat. She chokes, gasps and swallows some, and then chokes some more.

I keep her plugged until every drop is swallowed.

Dax is still rutting her as my softening cock slips from her mouth.

Her unhindered moans are wild and guttural as her head lowers, and her small fists plant against the forest floor. Gentler, now I'm sated, I lift her chin so I can see the rapture on her pretty face. Lifting her lashes, she boldly meets my gaze, her body swaying as Dax drags her on and off his cock. I'm on my knees before her, but she surprises me when she leans forward and closes her teeth over the muscle at my hip.

She bites hard.

My growl is low and steeped with arousal in seeing her mark me. Dax's hands have turned the flesh white where they are sinking into her ass. Her blunt nails raking over the exposed parts of my thighs is the sweetest kind of pain. My heart beats wildly, and I harden again as I recognize the significance of what she's doing.

Dax slows his thrust as she savages me with her small teeth, he's working the monstrous knot in and out. Her moans, as she grinds her teeth deeper, are filled with ecstatic joy, and her body begins to shake and convulse. Dax throws his head back and roars his release, rocking his hips against hers.

We're all breathing hard in the aftermath, and when she lifts her head, there is blood on her lips.

"I am claiming you," she says, her voice a breathy pant. "I claimed you first, long ago, but you are a proud male who needs the words. I claimed you first because you are first, but I'm claiming you again. You are mine now, and I will keep you until this earthly life is done with us. And even after, I shall keep you, and we will meet again in the afterlife. I have bitten you. Put my mark upon you. For all eternity, you are mine." She looks back over her shoulder at Dax, who is still locked in her cunt. "Both of you—forever and beyond."

Dax nods once. His eyes glisten.

She humbles me. This tiny Omega we have disciplined and fucked is neither cowed nor troubled by her lowly place before us. She is resplendent.

She is perfect in every way.

She owns and has claimed us all. Our lives belong to her now for all eternity, and my heart is filled with joy.

CHAPTER SEVENTEEN

Nate

I have scouted ahead all day. Silas is in a foul mood, and I haven't got the stomach to discipline Belle again today. If he asks me too, I know I'll challenge him for the first time.

Better he beat me bloody to teach me my place than I take my belt to her bottom again.

It doesn't help that she enjoys it, and then I'm denied the right to either fuck her or make her feel good when it's done.

I almost miss the fucking pigs, that's how badly I'm longing for a distraction from these troubles engulfing us.

As my wolf picks up their scent, I shift to human form. It felt good to have the loamy ground beneath my paws and the cool breeze ruffling my fur. It's helped to clear the troubles from my mind, but it's late, and the shadows that grip the forest are like a weight upon my shoulders. I know why he's angry—she claimed me, bit me, and declared her ownership.

Despite the repercussions, I cherish her words and wouldn't wish them unsaid.

I'm braced for trouble as our small camp comes into sight, but I'm shocked to find the atmosphere . . . happy?

The mutt yips and comes over to greet me, tail swaying from side to side double-time and body wriggling. I rub the wiry fur at the scruff of his neck while eyeing the camp occupants dubiously.

I'm convinced this is some trick, and the real Silas must be languishing in an otherworldly prison.

"You've been gone a long time, whelp," Dax mutters—he at least seems his usual grouchy self. He's eating mash, and my inner wolf immediately recoils. My attention shifts to Belle, and I'm pleased to see that she doesn't appear troubled.

"Silas is in a foul mood," I say, deciding to confront this matter head-on. "Who is this imposter?"

Dax surprises me by chuckling. He has a strange sense of humor. "He may be as dumb as the mutt sometimes, but he's got the measure of you, Silas," he says, grinning around his next mouthful of mash.

I sigh—I'm fed up with that nickname.

"I've claimed him," Belle states matter-of-factly.

Silas grunts, but otherwise doesn't rise to our baiting.

I guess he has fucked her, and it must have been good to have put him in this amiable mood.

"Does this mean I can fuck her again?" I'm pushing my luck, but I've not had my hands on her other than to discipline her since we left the village. My cock thickens in hopeful anticipation.

"No," Silas says. My eyes narrow in vexation, he's a mean bastard sometimes. "But you can sleep with her tonight, and tomorrow she can ride with you."

I'm disappointed that I can't rut her openly, but I possess skills in subterfuge, and I'm confident I will gain from this concession.

"Good," I say, nodding. "I'm famished. I'll go and hunt first."

I don't give them a chance for discussion, I shift and sprint eagerly into the darkening forest.

Belle

I've barely slept all night, and this is because Nate has found inventive ways to put his hands on me under the cover of darkness. Usually, he sleeps in wolf form, and his soft fur and warm body provide the perfect comfort, but last night he made an exception. His scent is all over me, and it's making me a little dizzy.

I'm exhausted and would like nothing better than to spend a day languishing in my little bedding nook at my old cottage while the fire blazes, lulled by the patter of winter rain.

There's no bedding nook, and the light rain is cold and falls directly into my face.

Nate, despite also not sleeping all night, is radiating perky energy as he whistles to himself. As I spoon the grim mash into my mouth, I pretend I'm somewhere warm and dry.

Despite my frozen state and lack of sleep, I'm needy to the point of distress. I'm hoping one of them will fuck me, but they are all business as they pack the small camp, and none of them appears interested.

I take my bowl and stomp off to the nearby stream to wash both the bowl and myself.

My mind is on neither of those tasks as I strip my gown and wade into the stream. It's freezing, and my teeth chatter, but I don't care. My neediness consumes me, and I'm determined to take matters into my own hands.

It won't take more than a few moments.

"Hurry up!" Dax calls.

I shoot a glare over my shoulder. Does he possess a cruel mystical awareness that tells him of my shameful intentions? "Do you want to fuck me?" I ask hopefully.

"Yes," he says, lusty gaze lingering on my ass before returning to my face. "But we don't have time if we are to make the town by nightfall."

"It won't take very long," I say. They have turned me into a wanton creature—I have lost every bit of pride.

His eyes narrow and nostrils flare as he slowly straightens. This small movement seems to emphasize the immense breadth of his shoulder. "Why are you so needy? What has Nate done to you?"

"Nothing!" My voice is a squeak, and my face must be a picture of guilt as he stalks toward me. I haven't yet felt the sting of his hand disciplining me in more than a tap, but he's a fearsome Alpha, and I know I'll confess everything that Nate did before he can land a single blow. "Someone always fucks me before we leave the camp!"

He stops a pace away. My feet are going numb, but I'm thinking about him rutting me from behind yesterday while Silas filled my mouth. Dax is the most intimidating male I've ever met, yet the thought of him putting his hands on me and his cock in me only makes me wet.

"Hurry up," he repeats, voice roughened. He makes no move to give me privacy as he stares at the stiff peaks of my nipples.

With no choice, I continue my cold wash while he watches my every move.

I'm shivering but a spell has me in its hold, and all I can think about is claiming Dax. Yesterday, I said the words, but I've yet to leave a mark.

I want to leave a mark.

No longer staring at my breasts, he's now meeting my gaze.

"Get out of the water, Belle," he says gruffly. "Before you freeze to death."

But I don't move. I *won't* move. I'm captivated by the brightness of his different colored eyes in the morning sunlight.

"Belle." His voice is a growl, but I still won't move. "Get out now."

We are engaged in a battle of wills. But I harbor a great well of defiance when it comes to getting my own way, and if he wants me out of the water, he's going to need to make me. "No!".

Dax

The little Omega is testing me. It's usually Silas who deals with her acts of defiance, and I'm not enjoying it. If I call him, as I should, he will tell Nate to take the belt to her.

I don't want him to punish her. I hate him punishing her, although I understand that it must be done.

But I need to get her out of the water before her small feet turn blue. To do that, I'm going to have to put my hands on her.

She wants to be fucked. I can see it blazing in her eyes, and in the stubborn jut of her jaw.

I want to fuck her—I've already admitted as much, and I don't trust myself to touch her in this state.

She smirks.

My patience snaps.

She gasps as I scoop her out of the water before throwing her arms around my neck and giggling. I growl. Somehow I maneuver us so that she's pinned against the nearest tree and have half-undone my belt before I remember myself.

"Fuck!" Her small teeth have closed over my throat, and the savage bite sends a shot of raw lust pooling in my dick. "Goddess help me," I mutter. She's claiming me, and I'm powerless to resist.

Yesterday, she said the words to Silas—a week ago to Nate. They both bear her mark, and although it will never take permanently with Nate, the meaning is still there.

The sting as she bloodies me is nearly enough to unman me. My cock is in my hand, and I'm lining the tip with her tight cunt as she growls over her prize.

Silas can slay me for all I care. I can't focus on anything beyond the need to impale her on my fat dick.

It catches the entrance, finding it drenched with slick. She's as sweet and generous with her body as she is willful and demanding, and I wouldn't change a Goddess-blessed thing.

"Open for me, Belle," I growl. The tip wedges in her tightness, but it's never an easy fit. I groan and grunt as I bounce her down onto my length. She's so fucking slippery but it doesn't help a bit.

"Fuck! I'm so fucking hard, I can't get it all in." Hands under her thighs, I bend her near in half, and using the tree as a brace, hammer my cock home.

Her lips pop off my neck as she slides down under my pounding. "Gods, yes," she gasps, head back, lips and chin covered in my blood, and eyes screwed shut as though in bliss. "Please Dax, I need it all."

I groan again. I'm a filthy beast rutting my tiny Omega prey against a tree, and she's begging me to give her more.

Wild with my hunger, I slam as deeply as I can—until there is nothing left to give. The wet slapping sounds of full penetration unhinge the last of my control, and my knot bulges, forcing me to slow.

My breath comes in harsh saws. She's a limp, delirious puddle in my arms, but my low growl rouses her. "Good girl, Belle. You're taking this so well. Come for me. Show me how much you need me to fill you up."

My palm closes over her mouth to smother her scream, and her hot core clenches around me.

I come, jerking and grinding her soft body into the tree. Legs shaking violently, I stumble a step back before sinking to my knees with her still impaled. Fisting her hair, I take her soft lips, my dick twitching and spitting cum until my drained balls begin to ache with the strain of finding more.

When I can drag my mouth from hers, I find her gazing up at me through lust-drunk eyes—she looks like she's been ravaged—what the fuck was I thinking?

"I'm double claiming you," she says. "The last time was not to my satisfaction."

I chuckle at her mischief, rousing a squeak from her as I crush her slight body to my chest with joy.

Belle

I'm feeling very smug—and tired—when we return to find the camp packed. Nate, still annoyingly cheery, lifts me up onto his horse. Shep is dancing about with energy I wish I felt.

I thought my time with Dax might lessen my neediness, but I think it has made things worse. "Can't I ride on my own today?" I ask. I can't take a day-long ride pressed up against Nate; his delicious scent will drive me to despair.

"No," Silas says. "And I want you riding up front where I can keep an eye on you."

I pull my cloak tight around me—I'm still a little flushed from Dax's attention and don't like the idea of Silas keeping his eye on me.

We haven't traveled very far when Nate presses his lips to my ear and says, "Lift your skirt, Belle."

My mind whites out for a stretched moment. We're a small distance from Silas and Dax, who ride behind. I can hear the soft drone of their voices.

"Belle," he repeats in a soft warning. "Lift your skirts a little so I can pet your pussy while we ride."

My heart is thudding inside the cage of my ribs, but I do as I'm told, easing it up far enough for him to slip his hand underneath.

At the first brush of his fingers, I start, and he chuckles. I have missed his laughter—and his touch—this last week. Last night's teasing has only made things worse. "You're soaked," he says, fingers strumming lightly over the needy bud. "I wonder why that is?"

My face flames as I attempt to wrest his hand away.

"Do you want me to keep petting until you feel good, Belle?" he asks, ignoring my weak struggles.

"Yes," I say too quickly, although I've just been ravished by Dax and should have no desire for more.

"Okay," he agrees. "But you must be very quiet or Silas will notice what I'm doing." As he talks, his fingers rub back and forth over the swollen nub and I have to bite my lip to stifle my whimpers. "He's not happy after what he heard you and Dax doing. He'll make me take my belt to your bottom if he finds out."

A small moan escapes my lips, knowing that they heard me only makes me more aroused.

"Hush," he says, nipping playfully at my ear. "Or you won't get to come."

I try to breathe normally, but the sway of the horse, and the casual way he slides his fingertips over the aching bundle of nerves, coupled with the fear of discovery, all conspire to have me rushing toward that glorious high.

He stops, and I want to beat him.

"I don't trust you to be quiet," he says.

"I'll be quiet. I promise." I would promise anything at this point.

His hand slides up, brushing my cloak open at the throat, and slipping the top-most buttons of my dress undone. My dress gapes, and he catches an exposed nipple between his fingers and thumb and begins to tug it gently.

"Be very still or he will know," he says.

This is the highest form of torture.

He plays with each breast, pinching and twisting the nipples before stopping and leaving me exposed for long minutes before he resumes the games again.

Somehow, I remain still and endure.

"Touch your pussy, Belle," he says, tugging without quite enough bite on my nipple.

I have never touched myself in front of them for all I contemplated it this morning. My cheeks are scalding hot, but I'm half mad with need, so I do as he asks. It's swollen and slippery under my fingers, and it's so pleasurable to touch it that I forget about being quiet until he clamps a hand over my mouth as his fingers squeeze sharply on my nipple.

The climax that crashes through me is intense, and his fingers don't have hope of smothering all the sounds.

The terror of discovery only makes me come harder.

He chuckles as he eases his hand from over my mouth and nips playfully against my throat.

I reach to close the buttons on my dress.

"Leave it," he says, voice dropping to a growl and reminding me that he's every bit as Alpha as Silas and Dax are. "I'm enjoying the view, and I'm definitely going to want to play again."

He does play again, but I don't mind.

And the day passes in a lighthearted way I haven't enjoyed in a while.

But then we arrive at the walled town of Anchoredge, the Imperium Guardsman on duty at the gate speaks for a long time to Silas while we wait. When Silas returns, I sense that something is wrong.

"He's been here," Silas says to Dax as he vaults into his saddle. There's no mention of a name, but I know instinctively that *he* is the outlaw, Oswold, who terrorized us in my former home.

CHAPTER EIGHTEEN

Silas

It has been a good day, and this despite suffering Nate tormenting Belle for the entire ride. I'm sure he persuaded her into believing that I would not know what was going on. But I would need to be deaf and blind not to notice what they were about.

It's payback for me not letting him have her all week, but she has claimed me now, and I'm more charitably inclined than I have been for a while.

Anchoredge is a small fishing town nestled in the forested foothills of the northern mountain range. A stout stone wall surrounds the town center, although a broader community of homes and commerce lies beyond.

We passed through here not long ago in our pursuit of Oswold, and the watch on the inner gate greets me. Dismounting, I join him. There is a small Imperium Guard presence in the town. The barrack houses a dozen of my brothers, most of whom are rotated at the turn of spring and autumn. This is the back end of the Empire, few aspire to linger for long, but the craggy guard on duty today has the look of permanency about him.

"We expected you sooner," the Beta says. "Slipped in and out of the city before we could react."

"Who?" I growl, although my gut churns with suspicion of whom he refers to.

"Oswold," he confirms. His eyes drift across our party but widen as they alight on Belle. "Is that an Omega?"

"Yes," I say bluntly. His focus shifts back to me, and he backs up a step before dipping his head. Word will soon spread. Omegas are rare prizes and that she has been thoroughly claimed by myself and my brothers, is a given. "How long ago?"

He scratches his stubbly jaw. "Seven days."

I nod. "We'll be leaving again tomorrow. I'll need to send a message."

"Yes, sir. Where should I send them?"

"We'll be staying at The Green Man," I reply.

He bows his head in acquiescence.

Returning to our party, I vault up into my saddle. "He's been here," I say to Dax.

"Fuck," Dax mutters. This isn't a conversation to be had in front of Belle. The damage to her innocent mind already caused by that thug is more than enough.

We ride through the gate and along the narrow cobbled streets where homes, stores, and shops of every kind are interspaced by taverns and the occasional church. Nate calls to the mutt who is excited by the new sights and smells, but is obedient to his master and stays close. It's busy but not crowded, and the turn to evening brings a chill to the air. Gas lanterns have been lit, casting weak illumination over the collective.

The Green Man is one of the better taverns to be found, and at this time of year, we are likely to find a room without trouble. The sign swinging in the light breeze has seen better days, the paint cracked and weathered in the salty air, but enough remains to identify the green, bulbous-nosed depiction of a man's topiary head.

I'm confident no one in this remote town has ever engaged in topiary, so who knows how it came about. It's a reasonable establishment, and better than taking Belle to the barracks, which would be the last resort.

A lad greets us in the stable, and another darts inside to forewarn the innkeeper of our arrival. There are scattered villages and towns between here and our home, but more often, we will be sleeping rough, so I'm happy to take advantage of a bed wherever I can.

Belle is pale under the weak lantern light, and I'm wondering if she heard anything of my conversation with the watch, or is simply exhausted from the climaxes Nate has wrung from her today.

"For fuck's sake, make sure you don't allow a wench to climb over you today," Dax says to Nate.

Belle glares at Dax. None of us are blessed with diplomacy, but Dax is particularly wanting in this regard.

A portly innkeeper comes to greet us. There is a great deal of head-bobbing while eyeballing the Omega until Nate, clearly tired of this, puts her behind him.

Not put off by this, the innkeeper tries to move so that he can see around.

"The room?" I say, drawing his attention back to me. He blanches as if finally realizing his rudeness, and with another bob of his head, shows us inside.

The rooms are functional with an outer day room and a double bedroom. I don't linger on the logistics of who will go where. I am first Alpha; it's a given I will get both a bed and Belle. The other two can fight it out since we can't all fit in one bed.

"What food do you have?"

"Fish pie," states the innkeeper proudly.

"Meat?" Nate asks hopefully, his wolf does not abide by fish. But this is a fishing village. If it doesn't come from the ocean, it's in short supply.

"Roast pork," says the innkeeper with a beaming smile.

Nate swears, Dax chortles, and Belle stomps off to the bedding chamber under the pretext of being tired, grubby, and in need of a bath.

The mutt follows Belle. He has an uncanny sense for trouble and often makes himself scarce.

The innkeeper glances between us in confusion. I glare at Dax, who is still chuckling. "Anything else?" I ask the innkeeper for want of a distraction before my brothers set about one another in this confined space.

"Carrot and swede mash," he says, although it's delivered like a question.

I swear I can hear Nate's teeth grinding.

The innkeeper casts a nervous glance Nate's way. "We have fresh mackerel or herring—the fish pie is always popular." The poor fool is anxiously wringing his hands.

"Bring us some of everything," I say, which is when the courier arrives, and the innkeeper makes good on his escape.

A bird is the fastest way to send news and the courier hands over the lightweight parchment to me.

"What are you doing?" Nate asks as I take the pen and ink and, trying not to overthink the words, write.

"I'm sending a letter," I say. Although it should be apparent even to Nate and his questionable intelligence.

"To Bram?" he asks.

"That would be the obvious conclusion." Although I am writing three, and only one of them is to Bram. The second is my backup plan—I'm not above using every trick at my disposal—and emotional blackmail—to ensure my older brother toes the line.

The last letter is to the Imperium High Command to notify them of my changed status.

"That doesn't sound like a good fucking idea."

Dax cuffs him up the side of the head. "I swear you are as dumb as the mutt sometimes." I hear the mutt whining from beyond the closed bedroom door, he knows we're insulting him.

"He's as responsible for her protection as we are," I say. "Oswold has been here—he could be waiting to waylay us on the road."

"I understand this," Nate says, full of belligerence. "But we don't know Bram's mind. He was born to rule, and he won't take this adjustment well. He will not submit without a fight."

"I don't fucking care," I say, my grin all teeth. "I wouldn't want any to doubt my claim as first Alpha."

The courier is listening to all of this in the manner of one who will soon gossip.

Nate's expression is doubtful, and now I'm the one feeling insulted.

"In other circumstances, I wouldn't doubt you," he says, confirming my suspicions. "But Bram has never learned to lead in the way you have. He is firstborn and arrogant. And should by some miracle he best you in a fight, he will never let any of us bed the Omega again."

I see Dax eyeing me. He's not one to show his emotions, and yet I sense he fears this too.

The little Omega has left an impression on all of us. She has claimed us as hers.

She hasn't claimed Bram, and his place in this is unknown.

Nate sighs heavily. "I want her to be safe," he says. "Informing Bram is the right thing to do."

His sigh and reluctance tell me he doubts my position as first Alpha. Today is one long line of insults!

The courier takes the sealed notes from me with a bow. No

sooner has the door shut than the one leading to the bedroom chamber opens. "Who is Bram?" she demands.

She is fully dressed and has clearly been listening at the door.

"It must be Dax's turn to punish her," Nate says with a sigh.

I crook my finger at her, and with a wary glance at Nate, who has made no move to remove his belt, she approaches me. I don't have the heart to discipline her for this, and snagging her waist, lift her onto my lap.

I've missed touching her, but Nate is right, and a first Alpha needs to understand that we all must share . . . as difficult as that is at times. She's still grubby and smells of sex in a way that no amount of stream washing can erase. Burying my cock in one of her tight holes is the highest form of pleasure, seeing my brothers take their turn with her under my command holds a different, but equal, allure.

The three of us have always been close.

Bram, not so much, and I can't readily say how I will feel about him fucking her.

I believe I will hate it.

I believe I will beat the shit out of him—maybe half-kill him— before I'm willing to concede it as an option.

And she, too, must accept him and claim him in the way she has claimed us three.

"Who is Bram?" she repeats.

As I look into her steady gaze, I'm reminded that this little Omega possesses a fearlessness that transcends her dynamic status.

"He is our older brother," I say. "And in a matter of days, you shall meet him for yourself."

CHAPTER NINETEEN

Bram

"My lord." My servant, Artis, enters my study, a letter in his hand. "News has arrived."

With a raised brow, I take the proffered letter, noting it bears our family mark. "Who brought it?"

"A courier, my lord."

Curious. Dax isn't a man who wastes time on pleasantries. Nate is little more than a whelp and more interested in scattering his seed as far and wide as the female persuasion will allow—which is wider than I care to consider.

Which leaves only Silas, the *favored* son.

I can think of no good reasons why Silas might send me a letter . . . by bird.

Waving the servant out, I put it on my desk.

I leave it there, studying it.

My lot in life is a coveted one, my family home and estate, substantial. My fingers drum against the arm of my stately chair. I watch as a fire blazes keeping the late autumn chill at bay. I contemplate tossing the letter into it and pretending I never received it.

My room is warm, and yet that letter leaves me cold.

He wants something from me, maybe even *needs* something from me.

A part of me enjoys that he might need me. Silas is not an Alpha who needs anyone for anything—a point he has made abundantly clear to me my whole life.

I sigh. It isn't easy to be firstborn and not also first Alpha.

Our dynamic is animal at its heart, and hierarchy is everything. It doesn't help that it's so unusual for those firstborn to not also be first Alpha.

It doesn't help that I would also be first Alpha in any other fucking household were my younger brother not so fucking exceptional.

If I'm honest, and I am that if nothing else, I'm also concerned by whatever the fuck this trouble might be for him to lower his pride enough to send a courier.

I'm still staring at it, and I am still loath to open it.

A sudden thought rocks me. What if one of them is dead?

I still don't pick it up and open it because I don't want the news of one of them being dead.

Yet, the note remains a possibility and an outcome that I'm not ready to embrace.

None of them send idle letters filled with pleasantries. There is no good to be found here; I know this. But I am firstborn, and I have duties I can never escape.

So with grim expectations, I take up the letter and rip open the seal.

My study door opens, and my mother breezes in, long silken skirts rustling. She doesn't believe in knocking, never did when my father was alive, and warrants me similar disrespect. There have been times when servants have all but spilled themselves onto my desk before me in a shameless invitation, but imagining my mother's shocked expression as she barges in is like a cold douse of water. I have often thanked the stars that I do not share Nate's propensity for fucking everything in sight because if I did, my dear mother would have found me compromised a thousand times over by now.

"Oh! You have the news too!" She points at the letter within my hand—the letter I have yet to read. Her face is beaming with joy, so I can only presume that no one is dead.

"Yes, I do," I say, trying to read the tiny scrawled writing on the thin parchment so I might catch up with this joyous news.

"Isn't it wonderful!" she says.

I nod, casting my attention between my mother and the parchment, and wondering at how I can be a man and an Alpha, and yet so thoroughly mastered by a tiny woman simply because she is my mother.

There is some consolation in knowing that none of my brothers fare any better in this respect.

Some, but not a great deal since they are the ones who have escaped this gentle humiliation while I suffer on.

She has turned away to stare out the windows, and I draw the chicken-scratched parchment closer to my eyes, feeling an irrational sense of superiority that my handwriting is far better than his.

"Your father would be so happy, bless him," she continues.

Yes, bless him, the man who spent a great deal of time 'happy' under other women's skirts.

"Omega," I say aloud. It is the first word I've been able to decipher, and a cold sweat washes over my body.

"Belle, it's such a pretty name," my mother continues, oblivious to the storm boiling my blood. "Do you think she will be pretty, too?"

"All Omegas are pretty," I point out. "But I'm sure her scent alone will drive me wild with lust, and I will want to fuck her even if she looks like the back end of a sow."

"Bram!"

"Sorry, mother," I say dutifully. The words are unraveling themselves to me, and as they do, my brain is regressing to a basal low.

They have claimed an Omega.

They are headed here.

They are in danger and need my help.

All these details are important, but I'm thinking about how her potent pheromones will be muted to other Alpha males, but how the combined scent of my brother's lust upon her body will have the opposite effect on me.

"Your father would be so proud!"

I grunt noncommittally. What does pride have to do with any of this? It's not as if they have engaged in a daring competition or heroic quest to obtain the Omega. They happened upon her and doubtless claimed her like savage beasts.

My cock thickens and lengthens, which is awkward given my mother is still within my study, and I force my mind to contemplate the back end of a sow to get the raging lust under control.

"You'll be leaving today?" my mother continues, like I'm not the lord of this estate and have no say in my plans.

I have no say in my plans. My brothers have claimed an Omega— I'm still wallowing in disbelief at this part—and their journey puts them at risk of a dangerous enemy of the Imperium, Oswold.

I know all about Oswold; I have a better-written letter from the King's advisor, warning of the outlaw's ties with the Blighten, who test our borders with the threat of invasion every year. I'm also aware, via this same advisor, that my brothers were tasked with tracking Oswold, which must have been when they found their

Omega.

An *Omega.*

Not only their Omega, but *our* Omega.

If I yield to Silas.

Or challenge him—I'm giving serious thought to challenging him.

An Omega is a rare prize, men have gone to war for less. I have not met her yet, but my bloodlust is rising.

"I need to speak to Hawthorn," I say. "Artis!"

My mother winces at my roar, and my ever-attentive servant hastens through the door.

"Bring Hawthorn to me," I say. With a bow, Artis retreats.

"Just like your father," my mother quips with no little amount of censure as she steps over to the door, long silken skirts swishing. "I must make preparations for her arrival. It will be so joyous! I wonder if she's with child?"

As the door closes on her retreat, I release the feral growl I've been holding in. Pictures on the wall shake with the force of it—I imagine my mother shaking her head in disapproval and nearby servants running in fear.

I'm a civilized Alpha, mostly, so displays of aggression unnerve the household.

As I set about pacing the confines of the room, the door opens to admit Hawthorn. He also doesn't bother to knock. "Interesting news, my lord?"

I growl at him. His lips twitch. He's also an Alpha, the commander of my personal guard, and the closest thing I have to a friend. My displays of temper don't trouble him.

"An Omega," I say. This is a vague statement, but the ability to articulate eludes me.

"Your mother informed sufficient servants between her day room and your study for the entire household to already know. I have begun the mobilization of our soldiers, and sent word to recall those on patrol to bolster our numbers . . . I presume we will be leaving to assist your brother's safe return?"

I nod. Words are like daggers in my throat, and I cannot get them out. My brother has claimed an Omega, which means he has rutted her through her heat. The note is short, but in that limited opportunity, he managed to also notify me that Belle had also marked and claimed him.

He was already the favored son, now he will be as a god among mortals.

"You're having difficulty adjusting to the news, my lord." Hawthorn surmises, his face completely deadpan. I narrow my eyes on the insolent bastard.

"Some," I admit. "I will adapt." I was ever capable of adapting, and my ability to do so is one of my few sources of pride.

My door is flung open once again—does no one think to fucking knock?!

My younger sister flounces in, dark ringlets bouncing, and cherry lips twisted in a glee.

"I hear Silas has claimed an Omega," she says.

"I haven't disciplined you enough in your short life," I say seriously, eyes narrowing. Priya is a tiny, pretty thing with flashing dark eyes that we both inherited from our father. She is also willful, petulant, and a source of constant strife. I had presumed she would reveal as an Omega and that I might have the opportunity to pass her on to a willing Alpha petitioner.

Alas, at eighteen, it hasn't happened, and few Alphas are willing to take on so willful a Beta.

It will cost me a great deal of money to be rid of the high-maintenance brat.

"He has. Do you not have stable hands to fluster?"

Her smirk drops. She's foolish if she thinks I don't know of the mischief and terror she visits upon every red-blooded male on my estate with her shameless attempts at seduction. It helps that they are all terrified of Hawthorn's wrath should they cross the line and bed her. Sooner or later, a fool whelp will be so beguiled by her fluttering lashes that I will have a scandal on my hands.

Not that I am personally scandalized by her sexual awakening, it is a natural, healthy activity that I would recommend to anyone were they not my ward and sister. But I will be damned if I'll allow it to make my task of finding her a suitor any harder.

I'm distracted from our glaring match by Hawthorn's growl. And more distracted that my sister blushes and lowers her lashes . . . although there is still a petulant tilt to her chin. I feel sorry for my friend that I have tasked him with curbing her activities.

Dragging my gaze from her challenging expression—she is clearly here to bait me—I turn back to Hawthorn. "How long before we can leave?" For better or worse, I'm resolved to the course I must take. I am yet to be over the shock, but there is a welcome distraction from my turbulent thoughts in action.

"By noon," he says.

"Will you challenge him?" she asks.

This is a step beyond impertinence, even for Priya. I'm ready to reach for the cane I've not used since she was a child when I catch sight of Hawthorn's locked jaw and clenched fists.

As I look between them, an epiphany occurs. Were I not so incensed by the day's events, I might even smile.

"Hawthorn, my sister requires discipline. We will soon have a young Omega joining our household, and I'll not have her first impression be that we are a family of discourteous heathens." Priya gapes at me, but I've reached my limit and have enough problems of my own to contend with. "From this day forth, you are responsible for giving her punishments fitting her behavior—I do not trust myself not to break our father's cane thrashing her bottom. If she harbors any respect, it is well hidden. I anticipate you will need to take a crop or cane to her daily, at least. Please instill upon her a thorough demonstration of what she should expect on our return that it might encourage her reflection on appropriate behavior."

I pause for dramatic effect before adding. "To this end, I give you complete autonomy to discipline and train her in any way you deem fitting or necessary."

Her naturally olive skin turns a sickly shade of white, and her eyes widen with shock.

Hawthorn's expression remains shuttered, but his fists have relaxed, and I surmise that he's not unhappy with this declaration and order.

I smile, but they're both staring at one another, and I might as well not exist.

"No!" Her delayed reaction is delivered in an unladylike screech.

Hawthorn, unperturbed, tosses her over his shoulder. "I will see to it immediately, my lord."

As the door slams closed on her wails of protest, I'm left alone.

The silence is oppressive, and all that is about to unfold rushes to the forefront of my mind.

I can adapt, I remind myself.

Then I smile again . . . for I don't intend to make it easy for Silas.

CHAPTER TWENTY

Belle

The warm room and bed I experienced in the town of Anchoredge are many days away. It is cold and miserable travel, and I'm sickened by the very idea of eating mash.

We are getting closer to the day I will meet the fourth brother, and it ties my stomach in knots. If Silas sees me playing with the mash again, he will order Nate to stripe my bottom.

I eat it, but I do not want it, and it settles a heaviness in the pit of my stomach as I think about what will happen next.

We have set up a camp for the night. The fire is small and gives off little heat. Nate is scouting in his wolf form, and Shep sits attentively, staring in the direction he left. I recognize that he has a new master now, but I don't hold a grudge about that.

I don't even hold a grudge that they tried to keep details of Oswold from me. I now know he is more than just a ruffian, but an enemy of the Imperium with ties to the dread Blighten.

What I am vexed most about is the discovery that there is a fourth brother who will also have a claim to me.

"It is but a small detail," Silas says. "This argument is pointless."

"It isn't an argument," I say, although I know that it is. "It's a discussion. And another man thrusting his hardened cock into me is not a small detail unless he is the only brother in your family who's not hung like a bull!" My eyes are spitting fire, and I'm daring him to say otherwise.

A tic thumps in his jaw. Despite my challenging tone and coarse word choice, I've no desire for him to spank me, or order Dax to spank me, or wait for Nate to return so he can take his belt to me.

I eye Dax, he's eating his mash, but I'm on to him now, and I know that he is amused.

"It isn't a subject men readily discuss," Dax says, "But I don't believe Bram is lacking. He would be comparable with . . . " His face turns toward his brother, who shakes his head in warning. " . . . Silas."

Leaning over, Silas punches his shoulder. It's a hefty blow, but Dax is built like a bull in every way and barely moves.

We are all distracted from the mounting tension by the return of Nate. He's in his wolf form, a dead rabbit is hanging from his jaw. I've seen dead rabbits before, but a short, sharp squeal escapes my lips when he drops it at my feet.

"Damn whelp," Dax mutters, thumping him on the side.

Nate growls. Dax goes back to his mash.

"It is a wolf thing," Silas says. "He's seeking to impress you with his hunting prowess."

"Oh," I say, feeling inadequately prepared for the magnitude of this gift. "Thank you, Nate." I stroke a hand over the thick fur at his throat. He seems to like this because he crowds into my space, knocking me onto my back before lowering his weight over me.

He doesn't remain thus but pushes his head under my skirts. I squeak out a protest and try to thrust my skirts between him and that sensitive place.

The puff of breath as he sniffs tickles.

Then he licks. The tongue is large and roughened and seems to find every sensitive fold in a single sweep.

"Oh!"

"For fuck's sake," Dax mutters. "If he tries to mount her, I'm wading in."

Nate, perhaps sensing one of them might drag him off, growls against my pussy.

I should be terrified by rights, but I can't find it in me to fear Nate, and the vibration is not unpleasant.

He shuffles back, escaping the confines of my skirts—and shifts—and in the place of a wolf is a naked Nate. "Hands and knees," he growls.

No one tries to stop him. Since I claimed them all, there is less tension between them. If anything, the lust of one triggers the others and all three of them end up mating me. My stomach pitches like I'm tumbling, and my pussy clenches over nothing, pushing out the gathering slick.

His eyes darken with need as they stare at my exposed sex. Between his thighs, his thick cock juts from a nest of golden curls, below which, hang his potent balls.

The intensity of his study makes me feel languid and heavy, and although I know I'm expected to obey, I can't move. His eyes travel up my body until they meet mine.

"Over you go," he says, tossing me to my hands and knees. No sooner am I in position than he spears me. The stretch of penetration is heavenly and welcome, and I squeeze around him in eager anticipation of the rutting.

Leaning over, he rips the bodice of my dress down and palms my small breasts. "Fuck, your pussy feels so good." He toys with my nipples, pinching them between fingers and thumb as he begins to rut me. Slow, deep thrusts that I use all my strength to push back and meet.

My focus centers internally on the sweet sensations as we slap wetly together.

Gripping my hips for better leverage, he quickens the pace, leaving me breathless and helpless to do anything but submit.

"I think I need the tight place tonight," he says, and my stomach does a flip flop that is somewhere between heated joy and fear. My glance back finds him looking to Silas for approval.

It is not the first time he has done this. Sometimes Silas agrees and sometimes he does not. Meeting my eyes, Silas slowly nods, and my stomach takes a tumble.

Nate's fingers find my wet folds, coating in the slickness before he spears two of them into my ass.

I groan as he pins my body tight against his, filling me with his cock as he fingers my ass. "Don't come yet," he warns. It burns. It will burn more when the fingers are replaced, but my pussy still gushes and flutters regardless. "Good girl. Let me open you up so I can get my cock in here. You're so tight, it always hurts a little, but this will help." His fingers probe deeper, scissoring, and stretching me. My confused pussy is drenched like this might help.

"Goddess, you are tight, but I can't fucking wait." I whimper as his cock takes his fingers' place in my ass. "Relax for me, Belle." I'm given no chance to relax—he never gives me a chance. Once the tip breeches that tight muscle, he grips my hips and works it in with savage thrusts until his hips are flush against my ass. It stings, and I struggle even as it makes my pussy and ass quiver with wicked pleasure. "A little more," he says, palming my cheeks apart so he can work it even deeper.

He begins to rut my ass. It burns, but I'm maddened by the need to be thoroughly filled.

"Please!" The sting has turned into molten heat and tingling that makes me quake and shake.

"What's the matter?" Nate asks like he doesn't know. "Do you need more? Do you need my brothers' cocks to fill you too? Such a perfect little Omega. Tell us what you need."

"Please, please, please."

"Tell us, Belle," he says. His voice has deepened, become *stern*, and it brokers no argument. It's the voice he uses when he takes the belt to me, and it makes me even wetter.

"Please, I need more."

"Beg," he growls. I don't recognize this man. Whenever he fills my dark place, he becomes demon-possessed.

I beg, over and over. Pleading with him, with all of them, to give me what I need.

When he finally drags me up so he's on his knees and my back is flush to his chest, I'm sobbing with my need. I barely see Silas as he kneels before me, hooking my legs around his waist as he lines up his thick cock with my entrance. My damp cheek is cupped in Dax's warm palm.

"Open for them," Nate growls in my ear. "Take their cocks nice and deep like we know you need."

They begin to thrust. Dax filling my mouth, Silas my pussy, and Nate my ass. My body is pushed and pulled between them, one and then the others, in and out. The sensations are complex and all-consuming. Hands and fingers are everywhere, pinching and petting, teeth nipping at my throat.

I am a leaf lost in a storm.

I am the center of an erotic interlude that transcends the earthly bounds.

A thousand butterflies dance across my skin. They sweep over me in waves.

The thrusts begin to change as they synchronize their sublime assault. They know me better than I know myself. My trust in them is absolute in this and all things.

It is too much.

It is not enough.

Their savage growls and grunts of pleasure and their potent scent act upon me as wickedly as their thrusting cocks. They use me for their enjoyment, but they give it back to me tenfold.

I soar.

My nails sink into flesh as do my teeth, seeking an anchor.

I am coming apart everywhere. My heart is pounding hard within the cage of my ribs.

The storm isn't done with me. I'm lifted higher still.

They empty themselves into me, filling me with their seed, and I accept it greedily.

I'm locked upon Silas's knot, but the others slowly withdraw from my body, although they don't step away.

They purr.

It's like a soothing balm over my sensitized flesh, invading me and comforting me. I'm still stuffed and knotted, and that beautiful sound is the last thing I hear as I fall asleep.

CHAPTER TWENTY ONE

Silas

Belle is subdued today. I wonder if we've damaged her with the rough sex, but I sense it is more than that.

She's worried about Bram.

We're all worried about Bram, but we are bonded, so it's hardly surprising we are picking up on each other's tension.

We are many days from the town of Anchoredge, the weather is turning sooner than we expected, and we've not yet met up with Bram.

I'm worried that he won't come . . . but I'm also worried that he will.

He was always the favorite son, but I can't believe my mother hasn't applied her indomitable will to ensure he makes the right choice.

There are many possibilities, though.

The birds might not have arrived.

He could have been waylaid.

He might have been elsewhere, and the news took longer to reach him.

I'm tense and surly today. The future is unknown, and the more days that pass, the more I worry about how the dice will fall. Belle is small and weak, and although she can be fierce and fearless, her body wasn't meant to endure days of hard riding and cold.

That we fucked her on the cold ground last night also doesn't fill me with pride. I want to blame the whelp, but I'm first Alpha, and I must shoulder responsibility for not bringing it to a stop.

She shares a horse with Dax today. The cloak we bought for her while in town doesn't seem adequate against the biting northern winds even with Dax's larger body blocking much of the whipping cold.

Nate rides at the front, within hearing distance. I can't shake the sense of foreboding, and I'm determined to keep him near.

"This is bollocks," Nate grouches.

If he was in easy distance of my fist, I'd cuff him up the back of the head.

"Quit whining," Dax growls.

"I'm not fucking whining!" Nate's rash explosions have gotten him a bloody nose on more occasions than I can count.

This moment has a certain déjà vu, but this time we aren't chasing Imperium enemies, and there is an Omega in our care.

Our horses plod on regardless of their bickering. The verbal sparring distracts me from the biting wind and threat of rain.

"The next village should be coming up soon," Dax says. "Keep alert, Nate."

"I'm always fucking alert! Don't tell me how to do my job."

We're all tense, it seems, and I don't have the will to tell them to shut up.

"What is bollocks?" Belle asks.

"Do not repeat that word," I say. "It's a cursing word, and you already know enough."

Unperturbed, she leans around Dax so she can see me. "But what does it mean?"

Dax is chuckling, I can see his body shaking with mirth. He might as well light a fire under her curiosity.

"It's a man's balls," Nate says. If he were close enough, I would bloody his nose for sure.

Frowning, she shakes her head. "That doesn't make sense, you weren't talking about your balls. You were angry about the situation. Also, I heard my father say it once when a nail slipped, and he hit his thumb with a hammer. He wouldn't tell me what it meant, either, and he never said it again."

"It is a multipurpose cursing word," I finally say since she is both curious and intelligent, and I can't find the will to take the strap to her bottom for either of those things. "It's not for you to use."

"Why not?" she demands.

I'm rethinking my decision on the strap. "It isn't something a good girl would say."

"I'm not a girl," she says. "I'm a woman that you have all put your cocks inside, and if the number of times you discipline me is any indication, I'm very rarely good. If you're telling me that I can't use the word because I'm a woman or a girl, that is ridiculous . . . and bollocks."

A tic thumps in my jaw. I swear she was sent by the Goddess to test me for a lifetime of uncharitable thoughts. I can't decide if I want to put her over my knee or put my cock in her naughty mouth.

"I agree with Belle," Dax says. "She is very rarely good."

Her gloating turns to outrage as she realizes what he has said, but our amusement is cut short when Nate lifts his fist in a signal to halt.

Belle

There is something in the way Nate lifts his fist that punches my heart.

Dax kicks his horse, and we thunder toward the trees.

A horse's wild scream pierces the air, but the world is rushing by in a jumble of slapping leaves and branches, and I can't tell whose or where.

My heart is an erratic tattoo in my chest, and my vision, tunneled. As we plunge deeper into the trees, more terrible cries ensue. The forest is thick with bramble, fern, and stringy saplings, and we are soon forced to stop. I'm half tossed from the horse before Dax jumps down beside me.

The horse rears. Dax thrusts me aside just as a sword whistles over my head.

There's a clash as metal meets metal, but I can't see what is happening because I'm scrambling to escape the horse's hooves.

Growls and hoots come from near and far. They have a viciousness to them that instills a sense of fighting to the death.

The horse snorts in agitation, stamping its feet, and I crawl frantically out from underneath.

As I rise, a body slumps to the floor before me—Dax is standing over it, bloody sword in hand. Fisting my arm, he drags me from the agitated horse.

"Is it Oswold?" I ask. My eyes are wide with fear, and I'm shaking up a storm.

"Yes," Dax says. "Him or his men. They are many."

As we escape the shadow of the horse, another man rushes us. Dark, ratty clothing, shaggy hair, and blackened teeth bared like a beast.

I scream as I'm pushed behind Dax. His sword becomes a blur, moving with so much force that it sweeps the bandit's blade aside and cleaves through his chest.

Blood splatters, coating me in warm, coppery stickiness.

More approach like a pack surrounding us, circling, but cautious of Dax's blade.

He's right, they are many.

A feral snarl is the only warning before a giant wolf leaps for the nearest man.

Nate.

They crash to the forest floor, the wolf closing his jaws around the outlaw's throat.

He shakes.

I hear the snap, and the flailing body falls limp.

The collective friend and foe—frozen in the wake of Nate's savage arrival—spring to action.

Two attack. Two flee.

But more dark-clad men swarm through the forest, and the world takes on a chaotic slant.

A dash of black fur passes me—it's Shep. Dax is fighting behind me. Ahead, Nate's head swings from side to side, jaws snapping at two men who poke him from left and right.

Silas is missing.

Shep has a man by the arm. He's a big, powerful dog, but he doesn't understand the danger, and the man is about to strike him with his blade.

Snatching up a branch, I beat the outlaw who dares to harm my dog. He grunts as the wood clips the side of his head and turns toward me.

Cursing, Dax pulls me aside before skewering the bandit. Powerfully enraged that the raider threatened Shep, I beat on his dying body with all my small strength until Dax snags my waist and drags me off.

"What the fuck is she doing?" Silas roars.

This distracts me and allows Dax to wrest the still swinging weapon from my fierce grip.

Shep is fine, I realize, and the remaining raiders are dead or fled. "Where's Nate?" I demand.

Silas storms over to snatch me from Dax, and kneeling before me, sets about examining me. I don't want to be inspected—there isn't a scratch on me—and I bat his hands away. "Where is Nate?"

His face is level with mine, and it is odd to see him at this angle unless I'm sitting on his lap. He has freckles . . . how have I never noticed this before? His dark eyes hold mine as he swipes his thumb across my cheek. I fear there was blood there, and I would rather not know.

"Having sport with the ones who fled. He won't go far."

A crashing comes from the undergrowth to my right. Shep yips in excitement long before the giant wolf appears, and I know it's Nate. He charges straight toward me, and I fear he will bowl me over, but Silas smacks his snout with the flat of his hand.

Nate whines and shakes his head.

"Dumb as the fucking mutt," Silas mutters.

Nate is still determined to get to me, and even Silas can't hope to stop the giant beast. The air leaves my lungs as I'm knocked flat onto my back before his big furry body pins me to the ground. The forest floor is sharp and prickly under me, but the weight is comforting. He nuzzles and nips at my throat, tickling me when he sniffs my scent.

"She's okay, lad," Silas says, patting Nate's flank. They fight and grouch with one another so often that it is easy to forget that they're also brothers who share a deep bond.

A bond that now includes me.

Nate told me once that he doesn't understand the human language when in wolf form, but that he understands the mood and sentiments of it. He shifts, but he doesn't let me go. Instead, he kneels, dragging my body against his.

"We cannot linger," Dax says gruffly.

For too brief a moment, I've forgotten everything.

The changing season.

The threat of attack.

And the fourth brother whom I have yet to meet.

The savagery of this interlude reminds me of my vulnerability, of all our vulnerability since our numbers are so few.

Yet of all the dangers, I fear this fourth brother most.

CHAPTER TWENTY TWO

Silas

Belle is pale and shaken after the attack and worried about the damn mutt who doesn't have a scratch on him and is too stupid to understand the danger we were in.

However, Shep came to her defense and deserves my respect for that. I rub the wiry fur at the back of his neck, and he melts into a puddle of gratitude, prostrating submissively, ears flat, and body wriggling with so much excitement that his tail performs more of a circle than a side to side wag.

The damn beast is growing on me.

Then Belle's worried about the horses, which aren't hurt either, only traumatized by Nate shifting too close.

Fierce protectiveness rises as I see her in Nate's arms. He is the youngest of us, sometimes I forget how young. Shifters like half-breeds less than humans do, and had my mother not been willing to take him in, he'd likely have been left to die along with his mother. The bond between him and Belle is different to the bond she shares with us. Nate is the one who mostly disciplines her . . . and the one who finds inventive ways to make her sweet body sing. When we take her together, it's nearly always Nate who instigates it.

Had I imagined such a scenario as our complex coupling, I would have imagined myself more jealous. This tiny Omega has a great capacity for love and carnality and needs more than any one of us could give.

It takes a good while for Nate to make himself let go and allow Dax his time to inspect the little Omega for damage. There is none, but there might easily have been, and none of us are happy.

It provides a stark reminder of why we need both Bram and the protection he represents.

As soon as we have gathered the wild-eyed horses and mounted, my morose mood returns. We are all on alert after the attack. There should be a village up ahead, but although it is better than sleeping rough, it doesn't offer much safety.

We've been riding for no more than an hour after the attack when Nate calls a stop again.

This time it's a pair of scouts for Bram's party, and my tension immediately spikes. Bram has stopped at a village no more than a few miles away to water and feed the horses, we are informed. One rider turns about and thunders back along the pathway to notify my brother. The other one is tight of lips and remains with us as we ride in.

No one speaks. Nate and Dax are equally tense, and even Belle remains quiet.

He came, and I don't know yet if I should be glad or regretful about that.

As the village comes into view, I see him waiting at the front of his men. They have dismounted in a small field on the outskirts, although a few villagers mill about. Either having a gander at the stately lord, coming to entice him to spend his coin, or both. He must have fifty riders with him, numbers that respect the Omega within our care. To Bram's right stands Hawthorn, the giant Alpha who has been our family Captain of the Guard for many years.

Bram cuts an imposing figure. His thick woolen cloak is lined and trimmed with fur and shields him against the frigid wind. His leatherwear is intricate and spotless despite his many days on the road.

He's a rural lord, and while I know he holds influence with the king, he is not a major player. Yet to Belle, he must have a barbarian king's grandeur.

As our horses pull up, we dismount. Belle is the first to find her voice. "He's your twin," she says with a note of accusation.

"Yes," I say, although it is painfully apparent that he is my twin since he is a mirror image of me . . . with resplendent leather armor and neatly trimmed beard and hair.

He is the mirror image of me, only better, I concede while scowling at the man in question.

"Do you intend to challenge me?" I ask.

He adopts a bored expression, which I'm loath to admit impresses me given there is an Omega in scenting distance, and he hasn't looked at her once.

I welcome him challenging me . . . but I'm also not looking forward to it. He is me, after all, and although he might not have seen the years of war I have.

There is a long pause during which the tension cranks up another notch. "Yes," he says.

"Why?" Belle demands with a mutinous set to her jaw. I would have thought after all the dick she got last night, and the subsequent attack, she would be less combative.

The little Omega needs a lot of discipline.

Bram's lips twitch as he turns to Belle for the first time. He has just said we will fight, that he won't yield, but that moment of humor takes away the darkest edge.

"Because an order must be established," he says patiently—I had forgotten how patient he can be, but he has been stuck with our mother and sister for the past years and will have received abundant opportunities to practice. "And because neither of us wishes to yield."

"I will always be first Alpha," I say.

His amusement shifts to me.

"And I will always be firstborn." His smile drops. "As to who is first Alpha, that remains to be seen. Perhaps I never wanted it badly enough before."

He is used to dealing with our mother and sister, but he's also used to dealing with the king and the king's advisors in ways that I, as a lowly soldier, am not. Bram uses words in the way a soldier might use his fists.

I know much of war and fighting, and I know that a person's mindset can win or lose the battle regardless of physical advantages.

And I do not have that much physical advantage over him. He doesn't have that much cunning over me. We're talking, but we are also preparing for what is to come. We are teetering on a knife-edge, and I'm less sure of the outcome than I have ever been, and I wasn't sure at the start.

"Now?" he asks, placing the decision with me.

"Now," I agree.

Belle

He doesn't seem like the monster I have been anticipating. He seems a lot like Silas, and not only in the obvious way he looks . . . A more refined and yet darkly barbaric version of Silas.

I don't mind that Silas is not refined, but I also don't mind that his brother is.

And he isn't a monster at all.

Yet, they have agreed that they must fight.

This doesn't make a bit of sense, but offering my opinion on the matter will only inflame the situation. I thought I wanted Silas to win, and for his brother to yield so that nothing would change.

I can see now that everything will change, no matter who should win.

I am young and have lived an isolated life, yet I believe that even if this wasn't so, the ways of men would still be a mystery to me. They don't hate each other, but there is a strained history between them, and I'm not part of that.

If Silas wins, it will damage the power that belongs to his regal brother. If Bram wins, it will damage the power that belongs to Silas as first Alpha.

I can see no path out of this that doesn't create damage, and I'm devastated to be the cause.

"I don't want them to fight," I say quietly to Dax. He's holding me, a thick arm around my waist anchoring me to him lest I cause mischief.

He sighs. "None of us want them to fight in truth, but it must be done. We are Alphas, and there must be a hierarchy—we have already explained as much. Without order, there would be constant conflict."

"He doesn't seem as mean as I remember," Nate says. "I think he will still allow us fucking rights."

Dax clips him round the ear. "Whelp, your foot is forever in your mouth. It's a wonder you take a step without falling on your ass."

The two men begin stripping off their weapons and outer armor, and my chest constricts as I fight the desire to cry. The man who challenges Silas is a stranger to me. I wish he looked different, that he was in some way monstrous in manner so I might find a reason to hate him.

I've spent a good deal of the time since learning of him hating him but now, as I watch them strip down to the leather pants, there is only a desperate aching in my heart.

This is wrong. How can no one else see that this is wrong?

Guards take the discarded clothes and weapons away before backing up.

They are alone.

My heart is like a hummingbird beating frantically in my chest as they circle one another. There's a fluttering hope that common sense will prevail and this will stop.

It doesn't stop, and as they clash, my chest stutters in a sob. Dax tries to pull me into his arms to shield me, but I won't have it. I'm sickened to my core, but I won't look away any more than I could look away when the outlaws attacked my home.

The blows are vicious and fast. I can't see much through my tears, but I see enough. The sounds are terrible, savage growls and grunts, the meaty thud of fists on flesh.

The sight breaks me as surely as their fists break each other.

The sky darkens. It isn't yet dusk, but it's like the Goddess herself is angry with their foolishness and is making her displeasure known.

Still they fight.

Silas

We have been fighting for a good while, and neither of us is gaining. There are moments when I think I'm gaining the upper hand, but then I realize I'm not.

He wants this.

As much as I do.

I push these considerations aside. I must be focused.

His face is bloody where my fists have landed. Bruises blossom across his exposed chest and arms.

I'm breathing hard, and I take little satisfaction from his beaten appearance, since I know I must look the same.

Swaying a little, he holds up a hand. I think he is about to concede, but then I notice that I'm also swaying and a breath away from landing on my ass. I hold my own hand up in acknowledgment, welcoming an excuse to rest and drink some water.

Hawthorn approaches with two water skins. His face is utterly expressionless. "I see you are as miserable as ever," I say.

"And time has not increased your wit, my lord," he deadpans back.

I'm somewhat mollified that he uses that respectful title, even as he insults me. It brings a tired smile to my lips . . . which hurts like a bastard since they are swollen and split.

Bram sits, which I want to take as a concession of weakness, but knowing Bram he uses it as an opportunity to conserve energy and is thinking to fool me into presuming he's weakening. The last few blows he landed suggest he isn't weakening at all.

I sit/collapse beside him—there is not enough pride in me presently to care how that looks. Hopefully, he will take it as a double-bluff.

Swilling the water around in my bloody mouth, I spit it out before taking a proper drink. Hawthorn, having glared at us like we are two errant children, strides off to join the troops.

"Will you yield?"

There is a lengthy pause where he appears to be considering this, during which my hope rises.

"No," he says.

"No?"

"That is what I said. Did I damage your hearing during the fight?"

"No, you didn't damage my fucking hearing. But now we must fight again." The surge of hope and the snatching of it away puts me in a temper I wish my body had the energy to use.

"Why?" he asks.

"Why what?" Now I'm wondering if there *is* something wrong with my hearing since he's talking in riddles.

"Why must we fight?"

He seems to be genuinely puzzled. This has to be the best triple-bluff he has ever played.

"Because there must be an order and a hierarchy."

"We could share."

"If we share, there will be chaos." I don't think he is triple-bluffing anymore, but I don't know what the fuck he is doing.

"Well, I don't believe so," he says. "We are two halves of the same. I don't see why we cannot share. I admit, I have fared better than I thought I would. I dare say you've had a rough night rutting the Omega, and that was why you were swaying on your feet and looking on the verge of collapse." I scowl at him, ready to toss the water skin aside and get to the beating part again. "I fared better than I thought I would, which should not surprise me since I'm the same as you, but different."

"You are not the fucking same," I say. He is firstborn—the favored son.

"I did not say completely the same. I said the same but different. Would you yield?"

"I would not," I say emphatically. "But I am first Alpha."

"Are you?"

The question throws me. And Bram is right. Our hierarchy is far from established. If I win today, it will be by a slim margin. That's not established, that is another challenge waiting to happen.

"Maybe we could try sharing," he says casually.

I'm confident this is him bluffing yet again, but I'm too tired to work out the correct terminology for a four-times bluff. "Maybe," I say. I no longer harbor a desire to fight. Just regaining my feet will be a challenge.

"Good," he says decisively, reminding me that he is firstborn and used to making decisions.

"Good," I reply, just as decisively.

He looks at me for the first time since we sat down, and his battered lips tug up in a smirk like he can see right through my fifth-magnitude bluff.

"What happens when we don't agree on something?"

"We will discuss it," he says.

"You can't stop them having their share of her. We will end up fighting again if you do."

He scowls at me as if affronted. "Why would I stop them? Is she not a natural Omega? Does she not take well to cock?"

"She takes to cock well enough," I say, feeling surly again. Ahead the troops are shuffling about, clearly wondering what the fuck we are discussing. I don't look to where my brothers and Belle stand. She didn't want me to fight to begin with.

She wanted us to share.

"Good," he says. "I look forward to introducing her to mine."

The bastard stirs a chuckle out of me.

He chuckles too.

"The whelp was worried you would deny him access."

"He's bonded to her?"

I nod. It seems we won't fight again today, and that we've reached an agreement of sorts. "She claimed Nate first."

"Well, that is unexpected, but I'm glad."

"So, you won't deny him?"

"Do you deny him now?"

"Sometimes," I admit.

"Then I dare say I will sometimes deny him too."

We both laugh again. I would enjoy it a lot more if the movement did not make me feel like my skull is being broken in two. "He's a fucking showman with her. Sometimes it's good to give him free rein."

"He has had a lot of practice," Bram says, and we both laugh again

Belle

They're laughing, and I hope this is a good sign, although I've seen neither of them yield.

I'm a little bit hopeful.

I'm also annoyed that they haven't come over and explained their decision to me, given it's me they plan to share!

"Why are they still sitting there?" I ask.

"They're old and need to have frequent rests," Nate says.

Dax grunts.

Neither of these responses is helpful.

Eventually, after my stress has reached a breaking-point, they rise from the ground. I'm worried they're about to resume fighting, but they return to the group of soldiers, where they dress.

When they approach us, I'm so nervous that I bury my face in Dax's broad chest and pretend they are not there.

The silence stretches. I feel the weight of their study . . . then *he* purrs.

I know it's Bram because they all have a different purr.

His is both familiar and yet different, and it encourages me to turn. Earlier, I met his gaze boldly, but now the mood has changed. I care deeply for the three Alphas who have claimed me, and who I have claimed in return, and Bram has sought conflict with one and all of them.

Yet that sound offers a balm over my jumbled emotions.

When I can make myself meet his gaze, I find the evidence of their fight in his split, swollen lower lip, and the darkening bruising that mars his temple and cheekbone. When I glance to his right, I find Silas looking much the same.

Bram holds out a hand to me, and Silas nods. This is agreed upon, then. I'm to go to the barbaric lord.

"Did you yield?" I ask.

"No," they say in unison.

"We've come to an agreement," Silas adds. "You will ride with Bram for the journey back to our home." Tension radiates from the two younger brothers who stand behind and beside me, but neither of them offers a comment. They are neither firstborn nor first Alpha, and a decision has been made.

"Why?" I ask. The new lord does not seem any more or less dangerous than Silas. "I don't know him."

"You didn't know any of us a few weeks ago," Silas says.

I consider myself to be good at arguing, but I can find no point of argument here. On the very first night we met, Silas stripped me naked and fed me while I sat on his lap—I had no say in that either. I understand the law and that this brother also has a claim, but I do not know him and it is hard.

"There are no more brothers lurking that I will suddenly learn of at a later point?" I ask, still feeling a little mulish.

The corners of Bram's eyes crinkle in a way that reminds me of Silas when he's amused but trying to be stern. It's strange to look at a person who looks so similar to one you already know, and yet not know them. "None," he says.

His hand is still held out, but there is no urgency in him. He is patient with me—more so than Silas, who wasn't patient at all.

There are no choices here. I must be brave, as I've been many times in my short life and, stepping forward, I place my hand in his.

My hand is swallowed within his. It's not as rough as Silas's, but it's not soft either.

But he's still purring, and this keeps my fear at bay.

As I take the step forward, I fall under his shadow. His rich scent envelops me as his body blocks the wind. Turning, he motions to the giant warrior who waits a pace behind. A warm, fur-lined cloak is passed over, and Bram drapes it over my shoulders.

"There, is that better?" he asks. There is a cultured quality to his voice, testament to the different paths his life has taken from his brother's. We have slept on the roadside, eaten mash made from grain or vegetable . . . along with whatever Nate could hunt. Where one exists in a world of richly furred woolen cloaks, the other is battle hardy and comfortable living rough.

I nod. The cloak is heavenly in its warmth. I've become deeply chilled as I watched them fight.

A horse is brought over, a proud beast with fine leather-working on the tack. I'm lifted up into the saddle, and Bram mounts behind me, a faint wheeze of pain reminds me of his recent battle with Silas

The others in the party are also mounting, and I twist around to be sure my mates will follow us, and that I won't be taken away. "Nate will ride ahead of us, and Silas and Dax behind. I will not separate you from them."

The tall warrior is still beside us, and he passes up a heavy fur-lined blanket. Bram drapes this over my legs, tucking it up to my waist. It blocks out all the chill wind, and I curl my hands inside.

"Warm enough?" he asks.

"Yes, I haven't been this warm for many days."

He growls, and I shudder as the sound brings a clench to my stomach and, lower, a dull ache.

The horse dances under us before walking forward to join the procession. A group of farming folk come to stand at the roadside to watch us as we pass.

This situation is strange and alien to me, but ahead, I can see Nate with Shep trotting at the side of his horse. Ahead of Nate are a dozen of Bram's soldiers. When I peer back, I see Dax and Silas, and beyond them, many more soldiers.

We're surrounded. For the first time since the fateful night when my cottage came under attack, I feel safe.

"You smell like sex," he says. His left arm circles my waist possessively.

"That is Nate's fault," I say.

"The whelp will never change," he replies. I'm surprised by the familiarity of that statement until I remember that they are brothers with many years of history that I know nothing about.

"He isn't a whelp, he's a man," I say, offended on Nate's behalf.

"I'm his older brother, and he will always be a whelp, even when he's fifty."

"You don't mean it as an insult then? It's affectionate?" I'm confident both Silas and Dax aren't thinking affectionate thoughts when they say it, but perhaps I'm wrong.

"I do mean it as an insult," he says, although I can hear laughter in his voice. "But it's an affectionate kind of insult that happens between brothers."

"I'll allow you to call him such, then."

"My Omega is magnanimous," he says, and I can tell he's still amused.

"I'm not your Omega yet," I point out.

"No," he agrees. "You are not. But soon you will be."

I have no answer for that.

CHAPTER TWENTY THREE

Bram

The tiny Omega has been riding before me all day. I'm hard as stone, and the combined scent of my brother's lust and her gathering slick has me near mad with need.

At times she is quiet and shy as she submits to my closeness, and at others, combative to the point where I wish I'd brought the cane.

Like most Alphas, I have little direct experience with an Omega, but this one is particularly obtuse, and borderline outright brat.

"I thought Omegas were submissive?" I say to Silas. We're inside my tent, camping for the night in a farmer's field—at outrageous cost. They see a hint of fine clothing and are suddenly bewailing their lot. Sick children, pig pox, and demon-possessed chickens that have flown to his neighbor's farm are tonight's tales of woe. I listen to all this patiently—I'm a patient man—before handing over the coin. I rarely get that level of creativity from a trained bard, so I consider it worth every penny.

"We got a defective one," Silas says.

My lips twitch as the Omega glares at him like she might attack him with her tiny fists.

I fear she may hurt herself beating on his larger form, so I grasp her by the scruff of the neck and land a sound blow on her bottom. She yelps, although I doubt she felt much through the skirts.

"She's not been disciplined today," Silas says. I do not ordinarily consider discipline a source of erotic interest—it's a chore that must be done where my sister is concerned. I am, nevertheless, deeply aroused at the mere thought of exposing her bottom to my hand. "It has been a long and eventful day," he continues. "She'll never settle otherwise."

"You can't discipline someone unless they have done something wrong!" she says, clearly outraged by this suggestion despite doing plenty wrong during the short time since we've made an acquaintance.

"We discipline her most days," Silas adds, ignoring her comment, which only serves to inflame her temper.

"I bow to your superior judgment in this," I say. "How is it usually done? I admit I'm a little out of practice."

"Nate," Silas says, thumbing in the direction of the tent entrance. "The whelp has some proficiency in this . . . he has surprising skills all round."

"Good," I say decisively. "Call him in, and I will watch and observe, and comfort her when it's done."

Belle

They have sent someone to fetch Nate, and I'm appalled by this decision. "This is bollocks," I say.

"Where did she learn this word?" Bram asks. His eyes narrow in a way that is all too reminiscent of Silas at his worst, but I'm being punished regardless so I may as well give them cause.

"Nate," Silas confirms. "But she knows plenty of worse ones."

"And to think I was worried about Priya being a bad influence," Bram says.

"Who is Priya?" I demand. "If she is another handsy tavern wench, I'll rip off her roving hands and use them to beat her with!" I clamp my mouth shut. This is how I ended up claiming Nate. I've known the new brother less than half a day but he's already acting upon me.

"Not a tavern wench," Bram says, drawing my body close to his chest, which rumbles with an alluring purr. Silas takes a step forward, his eyes have hooded, and I know he's thinking about fucking me. He likes my possessiveness, they all do. An Omega is a prize. That they have claimed me, and I them, is a source of arousal and satisfaction.

"She is our sister," Silas says, but I don't hear the words since I am crowded between two towering walls of Alpha flesh. His hand, cupping my chin, is bruised and raw. The face gazing down upon me with possession, bears cuts and bruising, too. He is a rough, primal mate, but the thumb that brushes my cheek is gentle.

He's not always gentle.

My breath catches. I'm dizzy and overwhelmed by their proximity and presence.

They want to fuck me—both of them, and as their scent rises, it triggers a reaction in me.

I want them to fuck me.

"How is she?" Silas asks, stepping back and breaking the spell, which is when I catch up on what was said.

"An even bigger brat," Bram says, but there is affection in his tone like when he called Nate a whelp. "She has reached the age where all she thinks about is chasing cock."

I can't say as I blame their sister, had I known the pleasure derived through a cock, I might have chased them myself.

"I have given her over to Hawthorn," he continues.

Silas finds this funny. Hawthorn is a giant warrior and Captain of the Guard. I know nothing of their sister, but I'm already empathetic and confident she is nothing like a brat.

The tent, while not overly large, becomes crowded when the flap opens to admit Nate.

He does not come alone, Dax has also arrived to complete my humiliation!

My bonded mates have ridden close to me all day. But Silas is right, and events have left me in a state of turmoil. I'm both happy to see them and nervous about what will come next. "Someone has been naughty again," Nate says, winking at me.

Dax strips me. And like that very first night when the three Alphas came to my cottage door, I'm given no say in how they handle me. My body is slight, and although they have been feeding me more than I've eaten in a long while, my curves are still slight compared to the buxom serving wench.

As I face Bram, he catches a strand of my hair between his fingers and thumb, studying it. "Goddess, you are perfect," he says. It's like a hook catching a tender spot deep inside my chest and giving a little tug. I'm not bound to him as I am to my three Alphas, but those words find the first chink. "Nate is going to take his belt to you now," he says. "I will hold you while he does it, and after I will make you feel good before we sleep. Silas will be with us all night. I want you very much, Belle, but there's no rush. I don't want you to fear I will do more than you are ready for."

I nod. I don't have a choice, but I'm glad that he won't take me tonight. He's right, I'm not ready. "Good girl," he says, and the approval of this lordly version of Silas brings a swell of joy. His big hand cups my cheek, and I find myself captivated by obsidian eyes that mirror those of his younger twin. He has seen and experienced different things, and these are reflected in the man. "Move your feet apart for me." His gaze lowers as he speaks. One hand still cups my cheek, but the other trails down the side of my throat, tracing my collar bone, before cupping my breast.

He's gentle, brushing his thumb lightly back and forth across my nipple until it buds and hardens.

I part my feet, widening my stance.

"A little more, Belle." His fingers skim over my stomach before the tips of his fingers pause against the red-gold curls. "I'm going to play with your pretty pussy while Nate uses the belt, and you will keep your eyes on me the whole time. Understood?"

I nod. I feel like I'm subject to the drugging effects of moon berries and struggling to draw air into my tight lungs. He's going to put his hands upon me while Nate uses the belt, and I'm so conflicted about what that means. My pussy, drenched from their presence and potent scent, is squeezing and pulsing with slick.

I hear Nate drawing his belt, but all my focus is on Bram's eyes and the slow ascent of his fingertips as they dip between my folds.

"Perfect," he says again, as his fingertips rub up and down over the needy little bud. It brings a whimper to my lips—I already want to come. But I'm also nervous as I anticipate the first lick of the belt.

I'm trying very hard to hold still, but I can hear Nate stepping closer, and my body won't follow my commands.

"Ah-ah," Bram says, taking a half-step forward and curling two thick fingers inside. "Fuck, your cunt is dripping." He pumps the fingers in and out, making wet, squelching sounds. "I'm going to make you feel so good once the discipline is done." He plunges the fingers deeper, drawing me up onto my toes.

My eyes widen, and then I squeal as pain explodes with the first crack of the belt. "Oh!" The pain makes me clench over his deeply buried fingers, and I flood with more slick.

"Eyes on me," he repeats, his stern voice cracking with all the force of the belt. My eyes fly open in time for the next crack of the belt.

Pain and pleasure explode, and tears spill down my cheeks. The sting of the belt heightens the erotic torture of gripping the thick fingers filling me.

"Oh, gods!" My mind flips between the different stimulations. I'm wet and slippery around him, teetering on my toes, and twitching violently as every strike of the belt sends arousal pulsing in my core.

"Eyes," Bram commands in a growl.

Focusing on his eyes only emphasizes the twisted pleasure. I rise up with every wicked strike, higher and higher, tears streaming and oh so close to that glorious peak.

"Enough," he says, voice sharp. The blows stop, leaving me hanging on the precipice. I burst into tears.

I cry harder when Bram withdraws his fingers and gathers me close within his arms before taking me down onto the fur-covered pallet bed. He purrs for me, and I bury my nose against his chest, clinging and begging for him to make this better.

Inside, I'm hot and throbbing. How is it possible to be this aroused and not find release?

Cupping the back of my head, he presses kisses to my damp cheeks, telling me I'm a good girl, and saying how perfect I am. But I'm inconsolable; I need to be filled.

Gently, and all the while purring, he rolls me onto my back.

I hiss as my hot bottom makes contact with the soft fur.

Then his lips close over the stiff bud of my nipple, and I arch off the bed. His palm spreads wide over my abdomen, pinning me as he licks around the stiff peak before sucking it deep into his mouth.

"Please, please, please."

I chant over and over, restless, and consumed by my need.

His lips pop off, and he stares down at me, eyes so dark they are almost black. "Open," he says. "And do not look away, especially when you come."

I nod. My chest rising and lowering in a breathless pant that stutters at the first brush of his fingertips. He's maddening in his gentleness. Lazy circles that skim over sensitized flesh before he dips his fingers inside.

The lightest brush of his thumb over my swollen clit and I soar, gasping and sobbing. He keeps up the gentle circling of my needy nub, rocking his thick fingers inside, and I keep coming over and over again.

"I need more." A stranger has taken possession of my mouth. I was sure I wasn't ready for this, but I don't care anymore. I try and grab his belt to free the rigid length pressed against my hip, but he catches my fingers with a chuckle.

"I have told you not tonight, Belle. But if you climb over me and feed me your pretty tits, I will play with your pussy some more."

CHAPTER TWENTY FOUR

Bram

The journey back to the estate is one of personal torment. The small Omega sits before me in the saddle. Her scent surrounds me, clinging to my skin and leaving me perpetually teetering on the edge of rut.

It doesn't help that she comes so sweetly . . . or the way she begs me for my cock.

I know the moment she sinks her teeth into me and claims me, I won't be able to help myself.

Her fidgeting rubs her bottom against my crotch. "Be still," I growl, pinning her against me. She knows what she is doing, little brat. It does not matter how often I set Nate to discipline her, the naughtiness does not stop.

"I need cock," she says—the little hussy hasn't a bit of shame.

"You'll get it where you don't want it if you don't stop," I say. I've used her pretty mouth often, but the relief is short-lived.

"I want it everywhere," she says. "So you make a poor threat."

Silas chuckles. He rides beside me. This is the longest we've spent together for many years, but even so, I've no recollection of him chuckling, ever.

"You're wasting your time trying to break her will. She has the rest of us whipped, I don't see why you should fare any better."

She sits up a little straighter, clearly pleased by his roundabout praise.

"You think you handled her better?" I ask.

"You can't discuss me while I'm here!"

"Hush," I say. "Or I will set Nate to striping your bottom for the second time today." She stills. It seems Nate has made an impression on her this morning for once.

"I did," Silas says. He can gloat since she has claimed him.

Claiming or not, as soon as we arrive at our estate, I will be burying my cock in the heavenly passage between her thighs that I have explored often with my fingers and tongue. Days of tempering my aggression and need to mate her, leave no doubt that I will be rough enough to tip her straight into heat when I finally fuck her. I will rut her, bite her, and take whatever action I deem necessary to ensure that she also claims me.

"I have better handwriting," I say.

Silas scowls at me.

"The note," I elaborate, wishing I'd not brought the matter up since I sound like a surly whelp, and Nate already fills that position admirably.

"When was the last time you wrote on carrier-grade parchment," he says. He ought to ridicule me for critiquing his writing given his Goddess-blessed attributes, but it seems I have hit a raw nerve.

I contemplate honing in for the verbal kill . . . one must take their victories where they can. "You are better at the fighting business," I concede. I have never bluffed so hard in my life as the day we fought for first Alpha position. Had he realized how close I was to my limit that morning, we would be in a very different situation.

"Not that good," he says, cutting a glance my way. It isn't a look of superiority, but a look of begrudging respect.

It stirs strange emotions in me. It is likely the imminence of rut addling my brain.

Or it may be that I'm only now acknowledging things I have buried deep.

He is my brother, my twin, and it never sat well with me that I should warrant special attention because I was born a few minutes earlier. I envied him the title first Alpha, and yet without it, we would have had no balance.

My father was not a charitable man, and that I failed to consolidate my birthright by also claiming the role of first Alpha garnered me his displeasure.

He's gone, but his ways have left a mark on us all.

Ahead is a familiar rise in the cobbled road. It's a cold and yet sunny day, and the trees are shedding, leaving a carpet of brown and gold.

I note the way Silas sits a little straighter in his saddle—we're nearly home. It has been years since he visited; the life of an Imperium Guard doesn't allow for idle time and visits to familial homes.

Once we crest this rise, the estate will come into view. A scout has gone ahead to forewarn my mother, who is doubtless driving the servants to despair with her preparations. I admit I'm curious about Belle's reaction. I love this home dearly, despite the strife I endured growing up.

It is mine, but it's also *ours* since the arrival of Belle into our lives.

I want her to be happy here.

To claim me.

To feel safe enough to nest so that we might get her with child.

So short a time ago, parenthood and family were duties looming on the horizon. Now they are anticipated, even welcomed.

We have all suffered in different ways.

Nate, the unwelcome begetting of one of my father's numerous affairs.

Silas, the second born Alpha who was forced to leave.

Me, the firstborn failure because I was not also first Alpha.

And Dax, who's quiet intelligence was overlooked because of his brawn.

And my younger sister, the brat my father doted on and who was cut most by his death.

The Goddess gives and takes—it is the nature of her work to find balance. Our Omega is a chance for stability, to have a family of our own, and bond together in a way few families do.

There will be differences of opinion, but it's for us to work through so that our children might experience life without the mistakes our own father made.

"What is it?" she asks, twisting so she can look back at me.

She's perceptive of my moods, even without the bond.

I smile. "We are nearly home," I say.

Belle

We're arriving soon. The knowledge makes my nerves flutter.

There are people here who don't know me. Strangers who will soon meet the Omega prize. A mother and a sister, and all the other people who must live in a home so large.

Ahead, there is a crest in the cobbled road, and I wonder at what lies beyond that looming horizon. Many days ago, when I was still living within my tiny cottage, Dax filled my imagination with stories of his home. I've never seen a real castle, but I have read about them many times as I followed the tales of the golden-haired princess.

The horse plods forward, its hooves clattering against the cobbles and merging with the clattering of many other hooves.

The procession before us blocks the view, but we are almost upon the rise when Bram nudges the horse into a trot, and we break free from the line.

As we crest the rise, buildings come into view, and he pulls the horse to a stop. Beside us, Silas, Nate and Dax also come to a collective halt, and we gaze down.

A small castle, Dax had said. But I didn't know what a large castle was and so an impression was hard to form.

It's not a small castle. It is a magnificent gleaming structure with towers upon towers—too many to easily count or see. Before it is sweeping farmland, and to the north, a broad winding river leading to a shimmering expanse of blue.

"The sea?"

"The sea," Silas confirms.

I've never seen the sea before but it is every bit as mystical and infinite as I imagined.

I am rocked.

By the view.

By my smallness against this vast world.

By my new understanding of beauty.

Beauty has always been the domain of nature. I didn't know that humans could make beauty, but as I gaze in wonder, I understand that they do.

As if by cue, they all nudge their horses to a gallop, and we race along the cobbled pathway. The wind whipping my hair.

I laugh.

We're finally here.

As we pass through the broad wooden gates where Imperium-liveried Guards stand on duty, we slow to a walk. They call out in greeting and bow.

Once within, I see that it's not one giant building as I thought, but a collection of structures that are a mystery to me. People call out in greeting to their lord—but they are all staring at me.

Nate

The long and testing journey has brought us to our family home. It has been five years since I left to join Silas and Dax in the Imperium Guard, and two since I last visited. My memories aren't unpleasant ones. I'm a half-breed bastard and received better treatment here than I would have within the shifter community. I've never been pushed the way that Silas, Dax, and Bram have, and that gave me the freedom to do as I pleased.

Shep is excited by the new sights and smells. As we dismount and hand over our mounts to the stable hands, I task a lad with ensuring the mutt is fed and bedded safely for the night.

A reception committee is waiting in the main hall, including a resplendent Lady Fran Wittner decked in her finest silks. She was never unkind to me so long as her husband's bastard kept out of sight.

Fires blaze on either side of the main hall, holding back much of the late autumn chill. It's late afternoon, and oil lanterns have been lit. Servants are faking busyness on the periphery of the room. I don't blame them . . . it was usually me sneaking about.

Priya gives me an impish grin—one that has gotten me in trouble on many occasions . . . and a good number of thrashings with father's cane.

Her smile drops before she is given a chance to be introduced to Belle, as Hawthorn addresses Bram. "My lord, if I might be excused to attend my duties."

I smirk. I've heard all about the duties Bram issued to him. I can't say that I'm sorry for my younger sister. As a child, she rarely suffered the same punishments as me—a lifetime of injustice is about to be redressed.

Her panicked squeak when Hawthorn stalks toward her, stirs an inappropriate chuckle from me. She takes a step back. Clearly, she had anticipated a reprieve given our arrival with the little Omega prey.

Priya's stammered protests turn to a squeal as Hawthorn snags her arm and tosses her over his shoulder.

I'd probably cheer if Lady Wittner wasn't looking so regally pissed.

We're all distracted by these antics, but as I turn back, I notice Belle, her face pale, her lips trembling. She's as sweet as she is fierce, and while she might have gotten used to us, her Alphas, this is a lot for her to take in. Her life has been isolated on a farm with nothing but a mutt, farm horse . . . and nine fat pigs for company since her father passed.

I still hate the fucking pigs, but they made her happy.

Her glistening eyes meet mine. "I want Nate," she says. A dozen collective faces turn my way—usually, I've fucked up when I get this much attention.

I glance between Silas and Bram because I don't know who has the final say, but I'm going to challenge them fucking both if they don't let me take care of Belle.

Bram nods, and since he's the one holding Belle close, I take that as final. I scoop her up into my arms, and she tucks into my chest. "Where?" I demand.

"Your chambers are prepared as requested, my lord," a bowing Artis informs Bram.

"Take her," Silas says. "We'll be up shortly."

Striding out, I take the stairs two at a time until I reach the west wing, where Bram's chambers are found. The tiny Omega in my arms has her nose pressed against my chest, her eyes tightly shut.

The door is thick and heavy, and I jostle her as I draw it open before kicking it shut.

His room is familiar, although I've only been inside a few times. A fire is blazing, and lamps bathe the room in a soft glow.

The bed . . . is not as I remember it.

Her lashes flutter open as I stop. "Oh," she says, tucking tighter against me, and taking comfort from my familiar scent.

My cock hardens and lengthens as I take in the huge dimensions. It is clearly intended to take us all.

Still fully clothed, I take her down on the bed, throwing my arm and the weight of my leg over her before closing my teeth over the juncture of her shoulder and throat where our claiming marks overlap.

I purr.

She struggles a little before I rest further weight on her, and finally, she settles with a deep sigh.

I think about the deep piles of pillows and down-filled comforters beside the bed.

Nesting.

I want her to nest.

A nesting Omega will breed.

My canines spring. Tasting her blood, I suck against the skin knowing I'm leaving a mark. She whimpers a little, but I've pinned her securely, and she has no choice but to submit.

CHAPTER TWENTY FIVE

Silas

"Well!" my mother says. "That could have gone better."

"We need to tend to her," Bram says.

I'm glad he's the one handling our indomitable mother. She never had the easiest life with our late father, but for a Beta, she gave as good as she got more often than her dynamic status might warrant.

She gives Bram a withering look, before bustling over to me and motioning for me to lower my head so she can kiss me on the cheek. Her lavender scent is familiar, and the tenderness in her eyes reminds me that although Bram is the favored son, she shared both her censure and affection freely.

Dax suffers the same when she bustles over to him.

I see Bram clenching and relaxing his fists as he looks to where Nate took our little Omega.

Seeing my smile, he narrows his eyes.

"I don't want to leave the whelp with her any more than you do,"

I say. "But he knows better than to test you when you're so close."

I'm talking about the rut. Her scent has been acting on him as it did on the rest of us when we first met. He's close to breaking—they both are—I think it's why she reacted so strongly to the situation. He wants her to claim him, and I know she will, maybe not today, but soon enough.

What she needs today is to be fucked, knotted, and bred.

I'm sure each of my brothers is surmising the same thing.

Bram represents the missing piece. We are at last in our family home, where it's safe for us to fully embrace an Omega in heat.

My mother spends more time than any of us would like with Dax—she always had a soft spot for him.

"We need to tend to her," I add . . . also, I don't trust Nate that fucking much.

Mother looks between Bram and me. "Which one of you yielded?"

"Neither of us," we say in unison.

She smiles indulgently. "I knew the two of you would see sense." And with those parting words of wisdom, she motions to Artis to attend her and bustles off.

Bram

On entering my chambers, I find our Omega on the bed, half-buried under Nate.

I've not seen her handled by my brothers other than the brief interactions where Nate disciplines her under my direction.

The sight is arresting.

I had wondered at this side of the relationship. Omegas are rare, and I've never heard of one being claimed by a single mate. Usually, it's brothers or closely tied Alphas who form a family bond.

Always there is a first Alpha who holds autonomy over her

discipline, fucking, and care.

We are breaking the rules with our unorthodox approach to her control. Silas and I are twins and too evenly matched physically for one of us to assert dominance over the other with any level of stability.

The care of an Omega is about more than animal instincts, though. Her safety depends not only on brute strength but on my influence and position in the political world. Together with Nate and Dax, we will care for her better than any other Alphas could.

A thin trickle of blood trails from Nate's lips over her collarbone; it isn't unusual for aroused shifters to extend their canines. In his younger years, Nate got into all kinds of trouble for marking up the bounty of willing girls before he learned to control it.

My aggression rises, seeing him marking her. I'm aware of their claiming mark. I've inspected it many times, thinking about how my mark would soon join the overlapping scars. She is restless under him. His worrying at that sensitive place will be stoking her arousal.

My cock swells. I want to beat Nate bloody and fuck her while obliterating the mark. My fists clench and relax, but Nate lowers his eyes and loosens his lock on her throat.

She whimpers as he licks the sting away.

Silas growls in warning—I'm not the only one struggling with Nate's possessive handling today.

"Undress her," I say.

My words break the spell of anticipation. We are all of us thinking about the rutting that is to come.

We all undress, stripping clothing as we watch Nate divest her of the dress, boots, and underskirts.

"Good girl," Nate says as he slides layers off, exposing her delectable flesh to our collective, lustful gaze. His hands roam over her under the guise of removing the clothes. Lingering on her small breasts, and making her gasp when he pinches her nipple.

My cock twitches as he gets his fingers all up into the wet folds as he helps her lift her ass so he can drag the last remnants of her dress down.

She is enjoying his attention, but she's staring at me.

At my growl, he understands that his games have reached their limit, and reluctantly relinquishes his position on the bed to me. She starts as I draw her closer, and closing my fingers over her throat, I take her soft lips in a kiss. Her moans are swallowed as I take the time to explore her. Our tongues tangle amid breathy sighs until my fingers tighten on her throat.

The roughness of my hold brings restlessness to my little prey. She is an Omega on the cusp of heat and aggression from a dominant male has predictable effects. I pull her off when she nips hard enough at my bottom lip to draw blood. Unmoved, I stare down at her, fascinated by the way her hips undulate against me, and her hands skim over my flesh with heated urgency.

My fingers biting deeper into her throat still her searching fingers, and a low moan of need pours from her parted lips. The claiming mark draws my attention. It's raw and oozing where Nate broke the skin. She's sensitive there, flinching as my fingertips skim the bruising.

Watching her face, I press my thumb roughly into the tender spot. She twitches, and her slim thighs press together. "Is that sensitive?" I ask. I know that it is, but I find I need her words.

"Yes," she says, catching her bottom lip between her teeth when I grind my thumb deeper.

Tugging her bottom lip from her teeth, I kiss her mouth again, my fingers sinking into the pulse points on her throat as I mercilessly pinch the claiming mark. Her small hands make fists against my chest; her body shakes and twitches with the onset of her heat.

She submits to my dominance sweetly, opening her mouth and letting me plunder it with my tongue. Her soft, little moans and restlessness only heighten my aggression. Before we are done, she will be thoroughly claimed and mastered by us all.

Her small hand lowers, and she grasps my cock, pumping it erratically, spreading the leaking pre-cum.

Our scent rises.

All of our scent.

My brothers watch. This one time will be mine alone to control. After, our little prey will belong to us all, and we will enjoy the gift of her body often, whenever and wherever we might choose.

Her fumbling attention to my cock has pre-cum trickling steadily from the tip. I drag my mouth from hers, and with a fistful of her glorious hair, direct her hot little mouth there. "You have made a mess, Belle. Clean me up like a good girl."

Grasping the thick length in both hands, she eagerly laps up the spoils of her attention as I roll on to my back and let her have her way. She licks and sucks all over it, pumping it when she has cleaned everything up to encourage me to spill more. I watch her with the lazy interest of a predator that knows he can take control at any point. My hand grasps her hair only loosely. I'm more interested in keeping it from spoiling my view then forcing her deeper onto my cock.

My shaft thickens under her hot lips, and her mouth plunges deeper, trying to take more of me than she can comfortably fit, choking herself with her enthusiasm.

She's a Goddess-blessed vision, this tiny sprite who pleasures me with her mouth, hips undulating as if to entice my brothers to fuck her.

I haven't watched them fuck her. None of us have fucked her since we met on the outskirts of that tiny village.

"I think she needs to be opened up," I say.

She moans, sucking me deeper and canting her ass in anticipation.

I have shared women before, and I have also enjoyed the attention of more than one. But now, and as I embrace the new life before me, it's the thought of plunging my cock into a well-used cunt dripping with slick and cum that holds erotic enticement. I had thought that I would want to claim her first, but I find the thought of watching each of my brothers enjoy her in their unique ways first holds much greater appeal.

That it will be by my command they spill into her adds a visceral level to the craving.

"Dax."

Silas growls, but he doesn't interfere as Dax takes his place at the foot of the bed. His cock is obscene in both girth and length. By the time he has taken his pleasure, she will be thoroughly opened and prepared to accept our combined lusts.

The bed dips under Dax's weight as his knee hits the feather mattress. Broad fingers make a dent in her flesh—the other hand slides back and forth as he plays in her soft folds.

She whimpers around my rod, ass jiggling encouragement that earns her a growl from Dax. "Be still, Belle." His open palm cracks as it connects with her ass cheek, and a pink handprint blooms as he pumps his fingers into her willing cunt. He works her roughly, his thick cock leaking a sticky thread of pre-cum.

With a growl of satisfaction, he lines up with her waiting channel . . . and thrusts.

His motion pushes her onto my length, and I growl as I slide into the hot tightness of her throat.

I drag her off by the hair, and she snatches a hoarse breath before Dax plows her again, sending her right back.

My eyes want to roll back into my head. The convulsing of her throat around my cock head is sublime, while the image of Dax plundering her with his monstrous rod is the highest order of debauchery. That this tiny, perfect Omega groans and pushes back for more is a source of fierce pride.

"Fuck!" Dax growls. "She is hot with her imminent heat."

He's a man of few words, and it's a sign of how much he is enjoying the rutting that she coaxes them from him now.

My intellect is sinking. I've heard tall tales of the rut, but never experienced one. Belle is like a rag-doll between us, pushed and pulled on and off our hard cocks as we sate our lust.

I will not last.

I cannot last. The need to empty my cum into her is an imperative that can't be denied.

She needs this.

Needs our seed inside her in every way so that we might thoroughly claim her.

I come. Her small hands were planted to the bed, but she grasps the base with one hand as she sucks my offering down. Her small tits sway. Her ass turns white under Dax's fingers as he tightens his hold and slows the pace—he's working the knot in. Her lips pop off, but I'm still coming, and it loops over her cheek and hair and upper slopes of her tits.

"Oh!" She can no longer brace herself against Dax's savage use. Her head slumps against my abs. The sticky, cum-coated fingers of one hand still grasping the base of my cock.

Dax roars as his hips lock against hers, his body jerking erratically.

Our little Omega is limp and twitching, and another jet of my cum spills as I see her stuffing her drenched fingers into her mouth, her face contorted in pleasure.

Dax rocks his hips. His massive bulk dwarfs her. I don't know how she takes his cock, let alone the knot.

"Good girl," Dax growls. "Keep milking my seed."

I see her stomach rippling with the contractions as I stroke the cum-splattered hair from her face.

She is a beautiful, broken mess, and we've barely started yet.

"It's not right," she says.

"What's not right?" I ask. There is just enough sentience left for me to suppress the urge to begin rutting her.

"Soft," she says. Her pretty eyes are glazed, and her pupils so dilated that the iris has disappeared. Awareness has gone; she's no longer Belle; she is an Omega who needs to be bred. "It needs to be soft."

Belle

My mind is drifting, and it's hard to hold on to thoughts. They slip through my fingers . . . my fingers are still sticky with his cum, and I stuff them into my mouth to get the last drops.

This is different from my last heat, and distantly, I'm aware that Bram was the missing piece.

"Belle?" The stern voice distracts me.

I blink. The civilized version of Silas has taken my chin between his fingers and thumb, and he is making demands of me.

I growl. My eyes lower, seeking out the hot flesh jerking between his thighs.

"Belle!"

My eyes snap up, my hand hovering . . . where was I going to put it?

"Soft." I say. I have said this before, I'm sure. There's something else missing, but I can't work out what.

"Here." Something is pressed into my empty hand, but my vision lacks focus. I blink at Nate before closing my fingers over . . . softness.

"Oh." I press my nose to the softness. It smells clean. It shouldn't be. It should carry my mates' scents.

The civilized Silas . . . Bram . . . is in my way. I push him aside impatiently and put the soft cushion where he was. Another one is passed to me, and I place it carefully.

I snarl at the male who dares to place one on the other side. He backs up, and I snatch the blanket up and put it where it needs to go.

I give in completely to my instincts. The bed grows thick and soft . . . and safe. It's safe here . . . but it would be safer if it was smaller . . . and more closed in.

I blink again.

They're watching me, four huge Alphas, their thick cocks jutting. I can smell their seed dripping.

They are wasting it, and that makes me growl.

Silas growls back, and my body trembles in response. His civilized twin stands beside him, but he doesn't look civilized any more.

I turn my back on them, and getting to my hands and knees, peer back over my shoulder.

They know what I need. *He* knows what I need. I want *him* to claim me and mark me.

But he doesn't give me what I want and need.

Silas

"Nate," Bram says.

Belle hisses. For once, she doesn't want Nate. Today, and now, she wants Bram, but he retains cognizance enough to make our little Omega wait. I understand what he's doing. He's taking the necessary actions to ensure she will also claim *him*.

My smirk is wicked. The Alpha in me is satisfied with his approach. She's our little Omega prey, and she needs strong, dominant mates. And as her body sinks into heat, she submits to us.

As Nate's knee dips the bed, she growls her vexation, turning wild.

Instincts are raging in Nate, and with a fistful of her hair, he pins the feral Omega to the bed.

"Bram!" She begs him to take Nate's place.

Bram watches dispassionately—he always had a dark side that he hid under his civilized facade. "Rut her," he says coldly. "It's what she needs."

Nate is a dominant Alpha in his own right, but he is neither first Alpha nor firstborn, and he understands it's his place to do Bram's bidding.

He takes her roughly, her glorious fire-tipped hair used as a means of control. Gone is the determined inventiveness that is so often part of Nate's interaction with our Omega. He is deep into his rut, and she's used for his pleasure, and his alone. That she enjoys it, is coincidental.

She screams as she comes, her stomach rippling under the savagery of her contractions as she milks his seed.

I take her next, and she fares no better. I tolerate no resistance. Demand her complete submission. Her pussy is hot around me, open and slippery with cum and slick. When she comes, it's the sweetest form of rapture as her muscles fist my cock and knot.

By the time Bram crawls onto the bed, she has lost all humanity. There are no elegant claiming words. She rakes him with her nails as she savages him with her small teeth, not lifting her head until her lips and chin are smeared with blood.

"Mine," she says. It's little more than a feral growl.

Fisting her throat, he puts her on her hands and knees and ruts her, refusing to give her his mark.

She begs and demands, turns wild, scratching, and railing at him with her small fists, even as she pushes her ass back to better receive his thick cock.

Still he refuses.

It maddens her.

Infuriates her.

But he's deep into his rut and will not be swayed by either her desperate, tear-filled begging or howling demands.

We fill her with our cum, feed it to her, smear it over every inch of her slight body.

She rises higher—we all do.

Our fingers leave scratches and bruises all over her pale skin, and when she is insensible with her heat, and her voice broken such that the only sounds she can make are the raspy groans of pleasure, Bram finally bites and claims her.

Her mouth opens on a silent scream, body convulsing in feverish climax.

I know with absolute certainty that our Omega has been bred.

CHAPTER TWENTY SIX

Belle

A week has passed since my heat broke, and I'm having a final fitting for a dress.

I now have ten silk dresses . . . that's more dresses than I once had pigs.

I miss the pigs. They are intelligent creatures for all they love to wallow in mud. I miss Percy too, the old farm horse that I have known since my childhood.

I'm grateful that I still have Shep, and my Alphas, who are now my bonded mates, are more than compensation. I blush, thinking about the wicked things they do to me whenever and wherever they get the chance.

"Does the dog need to be inside?" Lady Fran Wittner asks. She's not an unkind woman, but she hasn't taken to Shep the way my Alphas have.

Shep is currently laying before the fire of Lady Fran's dayroom with his belly in the air.

It is an unseemly position, but he's a mutt, and neither understands nor cares for a lady's sensibilities.

"He's warming his belly," I say. "He'll soon get too hot and roll over."

I stand on a small step while a seamstress fusses around me, clinching the soft fabric here and there and pinning for the final adjustments. The royal blue gown looks perfect to my untrained eyes, but it's not yet to Lady Fran's exacting standards.

"My lady?" The seamstress says. I turn to face Lady Fran, who passes her critical eye over the changes.

She nods. "She will not be able to wear that line for long now she is with child. Be sure to leave extra so we can adjust it."

My fingers twitch with the urge to touch my flat stomach.

I can't wait for it to start to swell.

"He smells," Priya says, her small nose wrinkling as though in disgust.

"Only a little," I point out. He found the pigpen, and I assume it reminded him of our pigs. The stable hand doused him with water after . . . it wasn't a thorough enough job.

Priya gives me a haughty look of superiority. It didn't take many days before I agreed with Bram's determination that she is a brat. I'm glad she has been given over to the stern Captain of the Guard, and I silently cheer every time Hawthorn collects her.

"He is half-wolfhound," she says, eyeing Shep like this is a failing.

Shep, ever attentive to being spoken of, rolls over and pads over to the naughty young mistress who has been insulting him. His tail wags—he doesn't understand that she doesn't like him. Impervious to her squeal of outrage, Shep places his big head on her lap.

"Goodness!" Her fingers have flown to her face, but when he gives her the impossibly sad dog-eyes, she tentatively lowers one hand.

"Oh, what happened to his ear?"

"An outlaw cut him," I say. "He was a brave boy and took a nasty slash to his thigh while defending me. Nate calls them his battle scars. He's a proud warrior now."

She pets the silky, undamaged ear, and his tail beats against the floor as he melts into doggy gratitude.

I smirk because Shep has vanquished the bratty miss. It's only a matter of time before she allows him to sleep on the bottom of her bed, and is slipping the greedy mutt treats.

The seamstress is satisfied, and I'm instructed to slip my carefully pinned gown off behind a privacy screen . . . like I care if someone sees me in my underthings, which are more substantial than the silken gown.

I'm helped into my day gown, which is every bit as luxurious as the one I'll wear to the planned feast, and when I return to the ladies, the door opens to admit the Captain of the Guard.

He bows to Lady Fran and me. Priya, I notice, has turned a pretty shade of pink.

"My lady, if Priya might be excused so I can follow my lord's instructions."

"What instructions?" Priya demands.

Ignoring her outburst, he continues to address Lady Fran. "The festivities are sure to over excite her. An additional discipline session will ensure her best behavior."

Priya's heated cheeks have turned deathly pale. I smirk. It is unkind of me, but I'm hoping he reddens her bottom, and she can't sit comfortably for the rest of the night.

"Bram would not agree to this," she says, her tone challenging.

Shep, ever wary of human discipline situations, slinks off back to the fire.

For the first time since entering the room, Hawthorn directs his cool gaze her way. "Your memory appears to have failed you," he says, eyes narrowing in a way that fills my heart with wicked glee.

"Your brother gave me complete autonomy over your care and discipline. An additional dozen swats with a crop while you repeat this back to me should ensure you don't forget again."

Priya's mouth is open, and her pretty face beet-red once more. She's desperate to chastise this impertinent man who seeks to tame her. Her mouth snaps shut as she recognizes the folly of such an approach. I have never experienced a crop, but I'm convinced it is the wickedest punishment the young miss could endure.

I'm very much enjoying this entertainment, and I'm convinced she will not sit comfortably for a week!

Hawthorn holds out a hand. There is a long pause before Priya places her smaller hand within—it is for the best, it's not unusual for him to carry her out to unladylike squeals if she doesn't submit to a civilized escort.

As the door shuts behind them, I turn back to find Lady Fran watching me, and I'm surprised to see she's also amused.

"I fear my sweet girl has met her match," she says.

There is nothing sweet about Priya, but I agree, she has indeed met her match.

I've never experienced a feast and have no idea what one might entail, but the entire castle has been bustling with activity all day, and I'm instructed to keep out of the way.

Today marks the end of winter. It's a profound change from this time last year when I grieved the loss of my father.

He would be happy with the way things have turned out. My place here, this home, and my Alphas might be considered a dream come true if I'd dared to dream so boldly.

I've enjoyed the luxury of a bath, had my hair fussed over by a kindly maid, Margot—who has quickly become my best friend—and donned the beautiful dress skillfully crafted to Lady Fran's exacting standards, when Bram comes to collect me.

Brushing the curls aside, his lips lower to the claiming mark that never fully heals. He sucks against the skin and a sweet ache blooms between my legs. "Greedy girl," he growls.

I am greedy for them all. They've been negligent today, and I'm feeling particularly desperate.

Tucking my hand over the crook of his arm, he escorts me down the winding stone staircase to the great hall.

The raucous sounds that greet us as we near the entrance archway remind me of the village tavern near my old home . . . only a thousand times louder. I send a worried glance Bram's way.

He smiles. "You're an Omega," he says. "A prize that men war over. People have come from far and wide to gawk. There is even talk of a visit to the King in summer." He pats my hand before winking at me. "But let us make it through tonight."

A great cheer goes up as I enter, and my nerves explode. People are standing; they all turn to face my way.

Then Silas is there on my other side, and the presence of both firstborn and first Alpha instills a sense of calm. They purr, and that comforting sound even though almost swallowed in the din, allows me to take the steps to our seats.

I'm in the middle, Silas to my left, Bram to the right, and beyond them, Dax and Nate. Lady Fran and Priya share the top table with us, along with others I don't know.

Food and drinks begin arriving . . . well, the food is new, from the looks of things drinks have been coming for a while. Everyone appears happy—this is wildly exciting.

I feel small between their towering presences. And safe, I am really safe so that even when a parade of people come to greet me, or 'gawk' in Bram's words, I embrace the moment although I feel shy.

I'm not shy. I have the heart of a warrior goddess beating in my chest. I have helped defeat outlaws, not once but twice, and yet this rich environment with its blazing fires and heavy tables laden with more food than I've seen in a lifetime, makes me feel a little woozy.

Wealth isn't a concept I'm familiar with, but as I sit amid these richly dressed guests who are paying homage to me, it reinforces my mates' wealth and position.

In my royal blue silken gown, with my hair carefully curled by my skillful maid, I'm a princess every bit as regal as the golden-haired one in my childhood storybook.

Many courses arrive, but I just pick at each dish put in front of me. Frowning in displeasure, Bram fills my plate with roasted venison and honey-glazed pike. It is delicious, but I'm too excited, and I can't eat.

Lady Fran doesn't stay for long, protesting that the revelry is the young's domain, she excuses herself for the night. After she leaves, the mood grows rowdier, and I'm soon hoisted onto Silas's lap.

"What are you doing?" I ask, scandalized. I'm already the subject of a great deal of interest, and this position will surely warrant me even more.

"I don't know how I waited this long," Silas says. "You've barely touched your food." He's looking at the table like he might draw a plate over and feed me. To distract him, I press my nose against the crook of his neck and give a little nip.

He sucks a breath in, and his hands tighten on my waist. He is distracted from plans to feed me, but now I'm fearful that he is thinking about feasting *on* me.

My fears are realized when his hand slides up the bodice to cup my breast. His eyes have lowered, and he's staring at the plump swell of my breasts where the dress has pushed them up. Breath catches in my throat as his broad, calloused fingers skim over the exposed skin.

"Keep breathing, Belle," he says, smirking. "There's going to be a lot more playing, and I don't want you passing out."

Despite his determination that I should breathe, I'm finding it very hard.

He chuckles, and my annoyance brings all the air rushing back. Beyond Silas, Bram has stopped, goblet lifted but not yet touching his lips. If Silas's face is hunger, Bram's is raw need. "I will not last through the fucking night," he mutters before draining the vessel and calling for more.

My focus shifts to the buxom serving wench batting her lashes at Bram. She isn't refilling his drink, she's shoving her cleavage under my Alpha's nose under the pretense of pouring his wine.

Silas nips my ear and pinches my nipple through the dress. Bram's head swings my way, and his hot gaze focuses on what Silas is doing. "Was she growling?" he asks, his eyes shifting briefly to Silas.

"No," I say. I wasn't growling, was I?

"Yes," Silas says, and I gasp when he pinches my nipple hard enough to leave a lingering ache. They look so similar, and yet they are very different men. Silas is a rough soldier who is open in his brutality and dominance. Bram might be confused with a civilized man—he is not—and that facade hides a man every bit as darkly dominant.

Bram grins. Leaning back in his chair, he goes back to sipping his drink.

I love them, both of them.

Then there is Dax with his dry humor, and who only has to glance my way to set off a flutter in my stomach.

And finally, Nate, the half-wolf shifter, and the one who disciplines me. A ferocious bringer of death in his wolf form, and otherworldly in his beauty as a man . . . he's as playful as he is wicked.

Silas tips my chin, meeting my gaze before taking my lips in a kiss that steals my thought for anyone but him.

At a harsh scraping sound, Silas lifts his head. My former seat has been dragged aside, and a servant is carrying it off. Bram has brought his chair closer . . . close enough for his hand to easily reach my thigh. "An Omega is meant to be shared," he says.

Silas smirks and returns his attention to me, capturing my lips. He doesn't have all my attention this time, though, because I'm also thinking about what Bram's hand is doing as it slides casually up my thigh.

CHAPTER TWENTY SEVEN

Nate

Now that we have all bonded our Omega, my place in the world is a different one. I'm an equal now—as equal as a whelp bastard can be.

No, that isn't fair to my brothers, who have never treated me badly because I have a different mother. They know our father wasn't always pure of mind or action, and they don't blame me for his sins.

So it is that I find myself seated at the high table, dressed in fine clothes made by the family tailor in a rush once the festivities were announced.

I'm not one for feasting, but it is the civilized thing to do.

Well, not that civilized, the hall is full to bursting with raucous laughter and merriment. Three fights have already broken out, and Lady Wittner has long since retired.

Semi-civilized at best.

There's a giant roast pig on the spit—Belle hasn't eaten a bit. I admit to not having the stomach for it either.

Those fucking pigs have scarred us all.

Belle has been passed between Silas and Bram for much of the evening since Lady Wittner retired. Her pretty face is flushed from their subtle fondling . . . there's a lot worse going on within the great hall. She's trying not to notice, but she is a naturally sensual creature, and it's having a predictable effect.

Bram is distracted by the arrival of a lesser lord, and I take the opportunity to snag our little Omega from his lap. My brother gives me a suspicious side-eye.

Whatever he thinks I'm about, it's likely mild compared to what I have in mind.

The lord is still talking, and to avoid being rude, Bram turns back to him. Taking Belle's hand, I slip into a side passage where the servants bustle past with more drinks and food.

"Where are we going?" Belle asks. She spoils her imperious tone by giggling. In truth, she doesn't mind what we do to her, and as often as not, encourages it.

"Shhh," I say as I dip into a little known alcove where I have persuaded many a girl to lift her skirts for me. I could take Belle to our room, or commandeer a nearby one and order the servants out.

This is more fun, though.

Using my arms as a cage, I trap her against the wall.

"Nate?" Her big blue eyes shine with mischief in the dull light.

My gaze lowers to where her breasts are pushed up to enticing plumpness by her skillfully crafted silk dress. I trace the neckline with my finger, smirking when she shivers.

One button, two buttons, and the creamy swells spill out.

"Nate!"

Palming them, I take her soft lips to keep her quiet.

There's a small struggle before she submits to my touch. "Good girl," I say as I lift my lips from hers. Her nipples harden as I pinch, pluck and twist them . . . and I know when I lift her skirts, I'll find her wet and ready.

"Someone may see us," she says like she's scandalized.

"I don't care," I say. We fuck her often. It's not unusual for us to order servants out of rooms so we might slake our lust, or get down to the business of rutting her and let them decide for themselves that they are better off finding other places to be.

Her lips pop open on a breathy gasp as I treat her nipples cruelly. "I can smell your slick," I say, and leaning down, suck one stiff peak into my mouth.

She moans, growing restless. I swear the more we fuck her, the more fucking she needs.

I hitch up her skirt slowly—anticipation is its own form of reward. When my fingers find her pussy, it's drenched enough to smear the tops of her thighs. My lips pop off her tit.

"Did Silas fuck you after your bath?" I ask as I pet the slick, needy little bud.

She shakes her head.

I smirk. "Bram?"

She shakes her head again.

"I don't understand why you're so wet then," I say as though confused. "It wasn't Dax because he was with me. Is it my rough treatment of your pretty breasts?" I nip the nearest stiff peak while plunging my fingers deep—she clenches and floods around me.

She is well-conditioned to our lust. The mere suggestion that one of us needs to rut her, and she's soaked and begging to be filled.

"I think I need the dark place," I say. "I haven't taken you there in a while."

"No!"

She tries to wrest my hand away. If one, or better still, two of the others have had their fill, that's the best time to take her ass when she is thoroughly fucked and too exhausted from their attention to work out what I'm up to.

But sometimes it's also nice if she's along for the whole depraved journey.

"What the fuck are you doing?"

Our faces swing to my right where Dax looms, blocking out the weak light.

I have my hand up her dress, her tits are out, and her nipples stiff and wet where I have pinched and sucked them. "And they call me the dumb one," I say.

As I relinquish my hold, she tries to snatch her bodice together around her breasts—they're swollen after my mauling, and she doesn't have a chance. Dax surprises me by plucking her hands away and pinning them to the wall above her head.

The movement thrusts her pretty breasts out like an invitation.

His eyes turn hooded as he takes one nipple between his thick fingers and thumb and rolls it. Her dress twitches as she presses her thighs together.

"What were you planning to do?" Dax asks, staring at her nipple as he toys with it.

"It's been a while since I had her ass." Dax's monster cock is straining the leather of his pants, and Belle is a restless puddle of need. It's been two days, but neither of them is inclined to argue with me about specifics.

"Okay," he says.

She squeaks out a token protest, but her protests work even less with Dax than me, and they don't work with me at all. His big hands disappear under her skirts, and palming her ass, he lifts her, pinning her against the wall as he frees his cock.

I don't think I blink as he spears her and bounces her on his length. She is gasping and biting her lips and trying to be quiet, which is hard because a Dax impalement usually makes her scream unless she has something occupying her mouth.

"Oh, goddess!" Her breathless gasp rouses me from my stupor.

"Fuck her cunt is hot," Dax says, dragging her from the wall and presenting her back to me.

"Fuck," I mumble, fingers clumsy as I try and lift her skirts and free my cock at the same time, and failing to do either of these tasks well. I'm trying not to think about how her ass will feel with Dax filling her pussy. It's going to be a challenge, one I'm literally up for.

Dax mutters a curse as I mash up against her back, pinning her slim body between us. "Goddess help me," he says gruffly. "She won't stop clenching around my cock."

I nearly come, and am a little rougher with her skirts than silk warrants—there is an unmistakable tearing sound.

"Oh please, Nate! You're ruining my dress!"

My chuckle has a dark edge. What we do to her dress is inconsequential compared to the abuse her little body will take when we both fill her up. Finally, I free myself and get enough of her skirts aside to find the little puckered hole.

She hisses when I press a finger in. "Fuck this is tight." Her slick is copious, and she is slippery enough for me to penetrate her easily despite the lack of space.

I pinch her ass cheek when she clenches. "Be a good girl for us, Belle, and let me work my finger in. If I can't do this, I'll have no choice but to force my cock in without any preparation. I don't want to hurt you more than I must."

She clenches again and tries to lift up.

"Hurry," Dax mutters. "She's greedy for it. For fuck's sake, stick it in before I empty my balls. It's not as if she needs any further lubrication, her pussy is gushing like a tap."

I pull my finger out, line up my cock—and press.

It doesn't go in more than an inch, and I'm not convinced the tightness is pleasurable. "Pull out a bit so I can get in."

"Fuck! She is savaging me with her small teeth," he says, voice rough with strain. "If I move, I will come."

"There's no fucking space." I dare not pull out even to gain leverage, so I'm forced to bludgeon it in another inch. Dax shifts, groaning with pleasure as he pulls out a little. It's all I need, and my slick-coated length surges deep.

I see stars. Somehow I manage to pull out again before Dax rams back in.

It's an ungainly rhythm. We're all close. Each of us chasing the dark rapture and transcendent connection that can only be found with a bonded mate. My hand fumbles for her tit, pinching her hardened nipple to distract her from what we do.

Our little Omega is well-rutted. It's obscene the way we crush her softness between our harder, larger bodies. She's helpless and has no choice but to accept our thick cocks using her tight holes. That our actions make her body sing only entices us to give her more.

My canines spring, and I worry at the claiming mark, biting and sucking as her ass begins to flutter. Our erratic thrusts slow, and we surge in together. My cock feels like it's being asphyxiated, but the puckered entrance of her ass rubbing up and down the length is sublime.

"Nummmmah!" Her squeals are muffled against Dax's chest as her inner walls spasm around me. I nut so heavily I swear my mortal soul exits my body. My legs shake violently, but I retain just enough lucidity to keep my knees locked. I can feel us all throbbing together as hot jets of cum flood her well-used holes.

Slowly, I regain possession of my wits. There is cursing, hissing, and complaining as we withdraw. My knot is still swollen, and I'm relieved that neither of us attempted to lock in.

She batters at Dax as he lowers her to the floor. He ignores her small struggles since it is clear she will collapse should he let go.

"My dress is utterly ruined!"

I chuckle. I don't mean to make light of the condition of her clothing, but surmise she's not damaged too badly if this is her greatest concern. I stuff my aching dick away and take over holding Belle so that Dax can do the same.

"Hush, Belle." I pull her against me, pressing her face to my chest and offering her my purr. She softens and allows me to help her straighten out her dress—it's only a small tear. Her cheeks, neck, and upper swell of her breasts are a pretty shade of red as I fight the buttons closed. It is a tragedy to cover up her beauty, but she's still shy, and parading her around undressed won't buy me affection.

"What is that?" she says, her face turning toward the hall. "Is that—"

Dax curses. My purr ceases, and I open myself to the bond only to be assaulted by a frenzy of malevolent impressions.

A scream cuts through the distant bustle of servants.

There is a familiarity to the terror of an attack.

It's the sounds of cockroaches crawling under your skin.

It's the rising of a nightmare as it creeps over a sleeping mind.

It's a single scream that becomes many.

I've experienced many such attacks as a soldier—I never expected to experience one in my family's bastion.

Dax curses again and, pinning me with a glare, pokes his head out of our hiding spot. "It's coming from the hall," he says, turning back. "Get her out of here."

"I don't have a fucking sword," I say. No one has a fucking sword because Bram forbade the wearing of them in the hall.

Footsteps are pounding toward the little alcove; we can't linger. "They're coming," Dax says. "Go now while you still can." He nods his head toward the kitchens. "I'll hold them off."

I draw Belle into the corridor. From the hall spill soldiers bearing the insignia of Imperium Guards. As I watch, they cut down the nearest fleeing servants.

They aren't Imperium Guards—not anymore. They have the

rough, unkempt look of Oswold's men.

"You don't have a fucking sword either! How will you hold them off? You should take Belle, and *I* will hold them off."

Dax rolls his eyes at me like this isn't the time for a discussion.

It's *not* a time for discussion, but it seems we are having one.

"Come with us," Belle pleads of Dax.

Dax's eyes drop to Belle before returning to me. It's the haunted look of a man going to his death, and it turns my guts to ice. "Your wolf can protect her better than I can," he says. And there is an indisputable truth in this. Turning his back on us, he issues a mighty roar before charging the soldiers.

"No!"

Belle's wail is enough to unman me. Terror and pain are locked into that single word. But I need to get her to safety, so I take her arms and drag her into a run.

Dax

I have no weapons and no armor, yet I'm charging recklessly toward a group of heavily-armed men. I think myself a man of reasonable intelligence, but there is very little thought going into this decision other than a need to ensure Belle's safety.

If my charge buys them enough time to escape the building that is as much as I can hope for.

There are four of us, and if one of us has to die to ensure she lives, that is the way of things.

I don't want to die. As I race along the corridor, I'm fierce in my love for our sweet little Omega mate, and I'm greedy for many more years with her. She is with child now, and if the Goddess is willing, that child might be mine.

But even if it's not, if she carries a little niece or nephew . . . or even if there were no child, she is the center of my Goddess-blessed life, and I would challenge the Demon Gods themselves to protect her.

The outlaws have stilled at the end of the corridor. For all they have the advantage of weapons, I will not make my death easy for them.

There's no time to consider what mayhem is happening inside the hall, or for the safety of Bram and Silas. Our Omega needs strong mates who can protect her, and we have done a piss-poor job.

My rage unnerves the soldiers clustered at the end of the hallway. Perhaps the feral gleam in my eyes—or my size—as I rush toward them triggers their flight instinct. Despite holding swords, they turn and flee.

They don't run quick enough or hard enough, and I take them down like dominos. The crack of the first one's skull as it hits the floor soothes my need for blood. His sword becomes my sword, and I skewer his companion.

Breathing heavily, I take stock. The bloody sword is poor quality and off-balance, but it's better than nothing. Ahead, I can hear the carnage taking place in the hall. My brothers are in there. Behind me, Nate and Belle are fleeing.

Nate is a formidable soldier, but as a wolf, he is death incarnate.

The decision of what to do next is taken from me as more men spill from the great hall, and I find myself under attack.

I fight. I have no choice. If I want to live to see Belle another day, I must fight.

CHAPTER TWENTY EIGHT

Bram

The whelp is fucking her. I try not to let this rile me, but it does. Not five minutes after he left with her, Dax also left by the same route . . . and from the lusty sensations pummeling me through the bond, I can only presume Dax is fucking her too.

Silas shifts in his seat before lowering his hand to adjust his cock.

"What?" He shoots me a glare. "I don't know what the fuck they are doing to her, but I've never felt this before."

"Something depraved," I say. I don't add that Nate is obsessed with taking her ass whenever he finds her weakened after one of us is done rutting her, and that I suspect this to be the cause of the extreme sensations plaguing both of us.

"He's been obsessed with her ass ever since we bred her," Silas says. "He was obsessed with it before, but it's definitely worse now. Perhaps it's a wolf thing. They're into ménage and there are only so many holes."

His beer-addled ramblings are taking our conversation in a disturbing direction. Dax followed after them . . . "If Dax has tried to impale her on his log at the same time, I will be—deeply unhappy."

Silas chuckles. "You've spent too much time in civilized company," he says before going back to his beer. "She's twice as needy since we got her with child. Knowing Belle, she's encouraging it."

I don't believe this for a moment, but it is fair to say there is a lot of pleasure flooding through the bond. We all enjoy her . . . together . . . separately . . . frequently. Our Omega has a generous heart.

Then there is the small matter that Silas and I have been toying with her for much of the evening.

Snatching up my wine, I lean back into my chair. The grand hall has degenerated. Any servers who do not move quickly enough don't make it back to the kitchens. Some appear purposeful in their quest to be ravished—it takes less effort to spread your legs than serve and clean, and, presuming the man in question isn't completely drunk, there might even be pleasure involved.

"The bond has quieted," Silas says.

"Yes," I agree. It's approaching time for us to make a civilized exit, and the other occupants of the room who aren't busy fucking are either becoming increasingly rowdy or sleepy.

I admit, I'm a little sleepy myself, but I'm sure I will perk up as soon as Belle returns.

"Fuck," Silas mutters.

There are many ways of saying that word—it is versatile, yet the way Silas says it brings me to instant alert.

A sick feeling forms in the pit of my stomach. I want to turn and look toward the corridor where Belle went, but eyes are on me, and I will give nothing away. My mind is churning in that heightened pre-battle rush of wild emotions that I have experienced few times in my life.

Silas has his hand under the table, distracting me from the hooded, armed men who crowd into the room.

"Where the fuck did that come from?" I ask when I see a metallic glint.

Silas grins—it's all teeth and aggression. "I'm a soldier first and last," he says as the first scream pierces the air and the hall degenerates into chaos. "And a suspicious bastard—which you should be thankful for. I had Nate fix a couple of swords under the table."

He shoves one at me. "Do you still know how to use it?"

"Of course I fucking know how to use it," I say. I take the sword even as I wonder at what the fuck two of us will do against so many armed men. But it's too late to wonder as Silas issues a battle cry before he leaps over the table and plunges into the fray.

I'm right behind him.

Silas

The hall is in a state of carnage. Tables and chairs have been overturned, food and the bloodied fallen lay scattered together on the floor. There are many enemies here, but their numbers do not deter me. Once, I was foolish enough to lay down my weapon, thinking it was the best way to protect Belle. Today, Oswold will have to prize my sword from my cold dead fingers.

I hack and stab, knowing that Bram has my back. He's no soldier, but he *is* an Alpha. As a young man, he trained every bit as hard as I did.

A commotion comes from the passage leading to the kitchen. Dax spills into the room, cutting down any who stand in his way. A ruffian is before me, our swords lock, and my fist swings up, connecting with his jaw. His head rolls back, and he slumps. My sword plunges through his gaping mouth.

"Where the fuck is she?" I demand of Dax as he wades through the nearby enemy to reach our side.

"Nate has taken her," he says, pausing to send a man flying as he swipes him aside with the back of his fist. The man sails for several paces before crashing into an overturned table. There is a crack of breaking bones and he doesn't rise again.

"You both should have stayed with her," Bram growls.

"I got cut off," Dax replies. "Where the fuck are all your men?"

"I do not know," Bram says.

But we are all distracted by the arrival of the outlaw's leader.

"Oswold," I growl.

"He is mine," Bram says.

"No," I reply, and I'm ready to beat my twin unconscious if he dares to interfere. "He is mine."

Nate

We are outside, but it's no better here. There are too many enemies and not enough of our men. There should be a hundred Imperium Guards within the castle estate.

Skirting the edges of the fighting, I pull her toward the stables. There is no safe place, but if I can get a horse, we can flee.

"Where are the guards?" Belle asks. "Are they dead?"

Her body is trembling, and her face is pale under the glisten of the moonlight.

"I don't know." I don't have time to worry about them now. I must get her to safety. The attack appears to be concentrated on the hall, and although there are people rushing past, we are able to slip into the stables.

The horses are wild with anxiety, but as I put my hand to the neck of the chestnut gelding, he calms.

I saddle him with haste. Belle helps with his harness, but she is shaking so severely it's a wonder she can fasten the buckles.

Tears stream down her face as I put her up into the saddle.

I'm about to mount behind her when a blazing torch is tossed inside the stables.

The horse rears, and Belle is nearly thrown off. Hearing the horses scream, the bandits attack, and my sword is fucking useless against so many.

The horse is wild-eyed and ready to bolt. I slap its rump. "Ride, Belle, I will follow."

She has no chance to answer. The horse is maddened by the flames, and my slap is enough to spur it on to flight.

I shift.

The first man crashes to the cobbled ground under my savage attack. My teeth close over his screaming face. A satisfying crunch accompanies coppery blood filling my mouth. I'm enraged by the danger Belle is in, and I shake viciously before casting the limp remains aside.

A growl rises in my chest. My lips curl to show white fangs.

The clatter of retreating horse's hooves distracts me from my quest for more blood, and my head swings to my left.

Belle.

Belle

Leaving the castle far behind, the horse charges for the forest. I'm not an experienced rider, and it's all I can do to cling to the neck of the gelding and pray that I don't fall off. The reins have slipped and hang low, but I'm terrified to lose my grasp of the beast's neck for long enough to snag them.

It will tire, I reason. Only it doesn't tire and the boundary of the nearby forest is looming close. Rushing blood and pounding hooves fill my senses, but there are other sounds, more distant, but gaining—the steady drum of other horses who pursue.

I brace as we reach the tree line. It's dense, and the horse, wild from the fires and fighting, plunges straight in.

It tumbles, and I'm sent spinning, weightless, dizzy, and knowing that pain will greet me when it stops.

The impact comes first. It robs me of breath and thought, and I wallow in this numbness briefly before pain explodes across my body.

I want to scream, but my lungs defy my need to suck air in, and I twitch uncontrollably, sure I'm about to die.

I—need—to—breathe.

The pain grows. It's like a raging entity that crawls over my skin in waves.

I must be dying. There's no other explanation. The Goddess has come for me, and I welcome her embrace because I cannot endure this pain.

The hoarse passage of air as it rushes into my lungs brings more pain—and relief.

Life isn't done with me. Still gasping, tears leak from the corners of my eyes. My hand moving to cover my flat stomach is an act of will alone.

Through the waves of torment, I hear the pounding of approaching hooves.

I will not be taken.

A cry tears from my lips as I heave myself to my hands and knees. Only now do I notice the sharp undergrowth beneath me and feel the stickiness trickling down my face.

My feet snag in the flowing, silken skirts of the royal blue dress. The small tear Nate made is of little consequence any more. My body throbs and aches, but it is nothing compared to the worry aching inside my chest for my mates.

Voices sound behind me: calls, cries and snarls.

Stumbling to my feet, I fall into a ragged run—distant sounds of battle come from beyond the cover of the tree-line. Instinct tells me I must hide if I'm to escape capture.

I stagger, stumble, pitch to my knees, and force myself to my feet over and over again. The world is coming through a tunnel, and all I can see is the next tree or sapling that I pass.

The forest floor is thick with ferns and creepers, and every step is a battle.

I'm being chased. I hear a steady thud of pursuit, but the beat is wrong for it to be a man. My head turns in slow motion, and I find I'm being chased by a wolf.

It's as enormous as a horse, fierce and beautiful in the way all deadly animals are.

My heart is racing, and I know I cannot hope to escape.

He takes me down, a slow tumble in a way that softens my fall. His weight pins me to the ground. The beast is strong, but I can still hear the battle, and fear makes me struggle.

Muzzle close to my ear, the wolf growls before its teeth close over the scruff of my neck.

I will be savaged, I'm convinced of this, but all he does is squeeze. The battle grows distant, and the pressure instills a sense of calm.

The wolf is not my enemy, I realize, he is my protector.

Nate.

Silas

Madness overtakes my mind, having Oswold in my sights. It doesn't matter that there are a dozen men between him and me.

I fight.

The hall's double doors crash open. It's Hawthorn, and he is accompanied by our guards. Blood-splatters his face and clothing—

his expression is grim. Where the fuck has he been?

With graceful efficiency and precision strikes, Hawthorn cuts through the ranks. Within minutes he and his men have subdued the invaders.

Hawthorne batters Oswold, pushing him back until there is nowhere to go.

A punch to the gut takes the wind from Oswold, leaving him retching on the floor.

"Belle was seen riding out," Hawthorn says. "Oswold's men are chasing. They have been paid well to capture an Omega for the Blighten. I've sent a dozen in pursuit."

The blood drains from my face. Breathing hard, I try to temper the rage engulfing me. Bram is storming for the door; Dax is right behind him.

I charge after them.

"Do not kill him," I growl as I pass Hawthorn.

The Captain of the Guard inclines his head.

Belle

I'm floating.

My mind is telling me that there should be something beneath me, but I cannot tell.

I'm safe.

"Ease up, lad. You're smothering her."

The voice is familiar, *Silas*. It releases me from the prison of my mind. A prickly forest floor is beneath me, and above me, a fur-covered body pins me to the ground. The weight is comforting, as is the sharp sting where Nate has closed his teeth over the claiming mark.

Nate growls.

"I will castrate the whelp if he does not get the fuck off her!"

Bram's voice lacks its usual cultured edge. He sounds stressed. I'm not stressed. I'm in agony, the likes of which I have never known before. But I'm not dead, and the only part of me that's not hurting is my stomach. I take comfort from that.

My mate's voices bring me the welcome news that they are still here. Whatever else has or will happen, I will take each breath as a gift.

But no, something is missing, and my sluggish brain plays catch up.

Nate . . . Silas . . . Bram . . . I have not heard Dax?

"Dax?" My voice is a croak, and tears begin to pool in my gritty eyes. "Dax!"

"I'm here, Belle," he says, and I set to sobbing in earnest as the furry mountain above me finally lifts.

Nate shifts. Strong hands gently lift me from the floor. "I want Dax!" The last time I saw him, he was running, unarmed, toward certain death. I need to touch him and reassure myself that he is all still with me.

There is growling, but as I blink my tears away, Dax kneels down beside me and lifts me so he can cradle me on his lap.

My head feels heavy, and it flops against his chest. "You are not to ever leave me like that again." I say. There is someone else kneeling before me, and gentle fingers brush blood-crusted hair from my face.

"I'm sorry," Dax says as Silas carefully inspects my face. "I won't do that again, I promise." His broad fingers spread wide over my lower abdomen. "How do you feel?" he asks.

"I hurt everywhere, but here." My hand closes over his larger one.

"She's exhausted and hurt," Bram says gruffly. "We should get her home."

As I'm lifted from the forest floor I look around. A dozen men surround us, horses waiting visible through the gap in the tree-line.

Nate is dressing in a pair of leather pants, but his worried eyes are on me.

"I want Nate," I say.

"She's not hurt too badly," Nate says, smirking. "I was worried for a moment when she said she wanted Dax that there might be some permanent damage."

Silas leans over and clips him up the back of the head. "Whelp, I will hold you down while Bram unmans you if you do not stop fucking gloating."

Wearing nothing but his pants, Nate makes his way to me. "I was so worried about you, Belle," he says. "All my wolf could think about was putting his body between you and danger. My wolf doesn't always think through the details."

I'm handed over, and I cling to Nate, but Silas, Bram, and Dax are also here, and I'm comforted by their purrs.

CHAPTER TWENTY NINE

Silas

We return to find our home in a somber mood. Lights blaze everywhere, and the merriment that filled the hall is long gone.

None of us want to be separated from Belle, but matters must be dealt with. Although she rode back with Nate, she's clinging to Dax again, and his gruff facade is softened by lines of worry.

"Take her to our room," Bram says to Nate and Dax as we enter the hall. "I will have the doctor see her."

"No!"

She's not happy to be separated any more than we are.

"Belle, you know we must tend to matters," Bram says in a tone that brooks no argument. "Return to our room and rest. We'll be with you soon, but first we must be sure that the threat is over."

Tears dampen her cheeks, but she nods and allows them to escort her out.

The two young Alphas who are Hawthorn's second and third

stand waiting while we finish our discussion. "What happened here?" I ask as soon as Belle is out of hearing. The hall is filled with the dead, injured, and those trying to help them. Tables and chairs lay in disarray among the bodies, scattered food, and drinks.

"They tried to take Priya," Caden says. He is Hawthorn's second, and his young face is flushed. "One of the guests—dead now—and a cousin to the king betrayed us. Riders have been sent to notify the king. This was not isolated. Word has come from neighbors of similar attacks."

"Where is our sister now?" Bram demands. "Our mother?"

"In Lady Fran's dayroom, and well-guarded by Betas."

"And Hawthorn?" I ask. I've seen the way he's been with Priya since our return. Bram made a good decision in that regard . . . he makes good decisions often, I'm forced to concede. But tonight has shown our security is poor, and that will need to be addressed.

"With Oswold," Caden replies.

"Why Betas?" Bram asks.

My head swings my brother's way before returning to the young Alpha. Yes, why Betas?

"The stress of the situation—Priya has revealed," Caden says, face darkening. "As an Omega."

Bram growls. He does not do so often, and many of those standing nearby take unsteady steps back. "Where the fuck is Hawthorn now?" Bram demands.

"Alone with Oswold in the cells," Caden says. "He ordered everyone to leave."

"Fuck," I say, but Bram is already storming off, ordering the two Alphas and a dozen soldiers to accompany us as we head for the cells. Hawthorn has taken to Priya in ways none of us could have expected. Now she's an Omega, it would explain much of what's been going on between them. And if the young Alpha's faces are anything to go by, they're part of this. Hawthorn will kill Oswold; I want to kill the bastard myself, but we need answers first.

When we reach the cells, we find guards at the entry—intended to halt anyone from entering . . . anyone but us.

Inside, we find Hawthorn splattered in blood, knuckles raw, and chest sawing unsteadily as he stands over the broken body that was once Oswold.

Bram punches him—Hawthorn doesn't so much as flinch. "You've overstepped your position," Bram roars. "This cannot go unpunished."

Hawthorn nods. He has the bearing of a man who doesn't care. I want to punch the bastard myself, but Bram is still the lord, and it's he who has been slighted most by Hawthorn's lack of discipline. I almost feel sorry for the poor bastard—Priya was bad enough as a Beta, I fear for Hawthorn dealing with her as a mate.

The beaten body on the floor moves and a weak cough follows . . . he's not dead yet.

"Do not try and keep me from her," Hawthorn growls back. He boldly meets Bram's glare, but his focus shifts briefly to Oswold, and his lips curl in disgust. His second and third stand a little straighter, wary, and yet harboring pride for what their captain has done.

"Do not test our friendship," Bram replies with equal heat. "I'll be the one to whip you on the morrow. You had better hope I've cooled off some before then."

"I'm hoping that you haven't," Hawthorn replies, his expression stoic now. "I deserve it. I would still do it again. Let me go to her."

"You will *not* fucking go to her," Bram says. "I would punch you again if I didn't think I would break my fist." He points at Oswold. "Did he offer anything or were you just beating him for threatening your mate?"

There is a pause while Hawthorn glares back, and I don't need the answer to know it was the latter.

"He did not offer anything," Hawthorn finally admits.

Bram drags fingers through his hair. "How did they even get her?"

"She was not in her rooms," Brook, says, copping a glare from Hawthorn that might crush a lesser man. The lad is Hawthorn's third and he shifts uneasily. "She was not happy about being sent to her room early in the festivities—she climbed out the window."

Caden lands a hefty blow on his shoulder. "Brook!"

Gods, this is a calamity, I'm confident we're all thinking about the thrashing her bottom will receive.

Bram waves to the two young Alphas. "Put him in a cell and don't presume to visit with my sister either, or you will find yourselves at the whipping post beside Hawthorn."

They have a mulish set to their jaws that says this is a poor deterrent, but they nod, and Hawthorn remains quiet as they escort him out.

The cell empties, leaving us alone with the remains of Oswold.

Crouching down, I fist his hair and lift his head.

He grins, teeth bloody, eyes swollen. It's a joyous sight on the sick bastard. "Where were you taking her?" When he doesn't speak, I press a thumb into a bloody gash on his shoulder. "Everyone talks and you're not dead yet."

He only grins as he lifts up a blood-smeared palm. "Not yet."

But soon he will be, I surmise as I roll him and see the blood pooling out.

"The Blighten are seeking Omegas," he says.

I shake him. "What for? There are no Alphas among the Blighten. What purpose do they have?"

He laughs. I want to take out my knife and carve up his face like he did to Nate, watch the tip slicing through his flesh over and over.

And I want him to talk.

But he is fading, eyes glazing even as I grind my thumb into his shoulder wound.

He is gone.

"Fuck!" My curse is a roar that bounces off the stone cell walls.

"This is not over," Bram says with a calm I wish I felt. No, he's not calm, his voice is drained, exhausted. As all of us feel. "I have reports from the king's advisor—this is only the beginning."

"I know," I say, and standing, ram the heel of my boot down onto Oswold's skull.

Bram gives me a look.

The crunch is satisfying. "Pity he's already dead," I say. "I'd have enjoyed that a lot more. You didn't see one of his ruffians with a blade to Belle's throat . . . or what he did to Nate."

"I'm sorry for all you've been through," Bram says, eyes on the carnage Hawthorn and I have wrought. "When I heard you had claimed an Omega, I admit, my thoughts were not charitable toward you. I thought only of how you would find even greater glory." His face is downcast; his expression sad. "You were always the favored son."

"I'm not the favored son," I reply vehemently. "And glory? What glory is there in soldiering? I've been at it long enough to be sure that there's none. You got everything." I feel the old bitterness surface. "I got nothing, even though I was first Alpha."

He huffs out a breath. "I did not get anything. Do you know what it's like being firstborn and not also first Alpha? No, you cannot," he answers for me.

The visceral nature of his words surprises me. He's not as I remember him—he's not as I *thought* him to be.

"I don't mind the way things turned out," I say. A year ago, I never would have suspected I might offer words of solace to my brother. "I don't even mind that this bastard is dead, only that I wasn't the one to kill him."

"I do not mind, either," he agrees. "And I'm glad you're a suspicious bastard who hides swords under tables."

I chuckle.

He chuckles too, but our amusement does not last long.

By unspoken agreement, we turn our backs on Oswold and leave the cell behind. We've people here who need us, and when the home is set to some level of right, there is a little Omega waiting for us.

EPILOGUE

Belle

"**B**elle!"

My entire being jumps at that roar. Even Shep whines and pins his ears down in shame.

"Put some fucking shoes on!"

I glance down at my bare feet. Avoiding Lady Fran has become a thing. She is well-meaning but fussy and still not keen on Shep. Also, Priya *has* taken to Shep, and the only way the pair of us get any peace is to hide in my chamber. Here Shep gets to lounge beside me on the bed while I read a book I found in Bram's library. Shoes are not a priority. "Shep needs to go," I say.

"The damn mutt can find his own way," Silas says. He's still stalking toward me, and I'm torn between a desire to flee, and righteous indignation.

"You cannot discipline me," I say, because he wears the look of a man thinking about discipline. Now I'm pregnant the discipline has stopped, although I would never admit to my mates, on occasion I do miss Nate and his belt.

"Is that so," he says, eyes narrowing in a way that tightens my chest and ties my tummy in knots.

It's not fear exactly. I'm a little nervous—he's a fearsome mate, but the sensations that consume me are the unmistakable ones of love.

At times I feel like my small body cannot contain all the love and joy, and I'm sure that I will burst.

"There are many ways to discipline an Omega," he says ominously, rousing me from pleasant daydreams.

Shep, sensing trouble, slinks off. In truth, he does know his way out, usually via the kitchen where the servants are wont to offer him treats. That he bears the scars acquired while defending me earns him the fierce respect of everyone here.

"What ways?" I ask. I don't know what deviant plans he's hatching, but I'm sure I won't like a single one.

"Why doesn't she have any shoes on?"

My head swings around to find Bram approaching from behind. His scowl, coupled with that purposeful stride, start a flutter low in my belly.

They are so similar and yet as different as night and day. The civilized one holds his darkness deep inside, while Silas is rough and blunt.

"She's suffering from a lack of discipline," Silas says.

I try and dart around him—this conversation is not going to my liking, but Silas snags my waist. A nervous tension envelops me as Bram closes in, and I find myself trapped between two walls of Alpha flesh.

"You can't discipline me," I repeat, but I'm not feeling confident anymore. They're staring at each other over the top of my head while engaging in silent communication.

Scheming is the word that comes to mind.

"Hush," Bram says, closing his hand over my nape. I shudder at the feeling of his warm, slightly calloused fingers touching me. "You know we would never do anything to harm you or the babe . . . but you'll be feeling suitably repentant before we are done."

I've only vague memories of my heat but retain a strong impression that Bram revealed his most wicked side.

"Naughty little Omegas who misbehave don't deserve to feel good," he adds.

"I'm sorry about the shoes," I say, although I fear this admission is too little too late.

Bram squeezes his fingers slightly, and it brings a hitch to my breath. His thumb brushes up and down the column of my throat.

Silas chuckles. I glare up at him, but it only amuses him more.

"What about the others?" Silas asks.

"Not today," Bram says decisively. "Today, our little Omega prey is all ours."

But before we can enter our chamber, other footsteps approach.

"Who let the mutt out?" Nate demands. "He rolled in the pigpen and then shook himself all over Dax."

I giggle seeing Dax right behind him, face thunderous, minus a shirt and dripping water everywhere.

"It's like we are all lads again," Bram says with a huff. "They have a sixth-sense for missing out on a treat."

Nate smirks as he barges between them, scoops me up, and carries me into the room. "Some treats are better shared," he says as he winks at me.

I am taken to the giant bed thick with pillows, cushions, and soft blankets that make the perfect nest. Here they tease me, driving me to the brink of climax only to make me wait. It's a harsh punishment, and I would much rather take the swift pain of the belt.

By the time they are done tormenting me and allow me to find release, my entire body is engulfed in hot pinpricks, and I come with a scream.

Afterwards, I float in a hazy bliss. Distantly, I'm aware of Silas and Bram leaving, of Nate shifting to his wolf form so he can nap behind me, and of Dax's warm chest under my cheek.

I am content. My body still tingles from what they've done, and a pleasant ache emanates between my thighs.

My mind drifts, as it often does, to a world of adventure. The princess in my children's book has blonde hair, mine is dark red, but today the heroine is different. This one has dark ringleted hair and flashing brown eyes. She is a naughty, willful Omega, and she causes no end of mischief for her mates.

She stands on the prow of a great wooden ship. A red wolf head flag flutters on the high mast overhead. Seagulls are circling, cawing as they ride the warm currents. Ahead is a shoreline with buildings in shades of brown and grey jutting unevenly toward the sky.

Footsteps are approaching, a heavy, even tread, and I press my nose deeper against the safety of Dax's chest as the dream draws me in.

She turns, her haughty expression declaring her irritation with the male who dares to interrupt her.

The brooding Alpha only smirks. Long, dark hair tied back in a cue, a rough beard, and a fearsome scar that dissects his right brow and cheek.

I recognize the miss. The man who claims her lips, I do not.

ABOUT THE AUTHOR

I love a happily ever after, although sometimes the journey to get there can be rough on my poor characters.

An unashamed fan of the alpha, the antihero, and the throwback in all his guises and wherever he may lurk.

I'm a new author, learning as I go and appreciate feedback of all kinds.

Drop me a message and let me know what you think.

Website: www.authorlvlane.com
Facebook Page: www.facebook.com/LVLaneAuthor/
Facebook group: www.facebook.com/groups/LVLane/
Goodreads: www.goodreads.com/LVLane
Amazon: www.amazon.com/author/lvlane

Printed in Great Britain
by Amazon